For a hot second she h... to do nothing.

To just let the man who'd been targeting her die in the hope that the threat would depart with him. But Teresa just couldn't let another human being die.

Matt must have sensed her upset, since he rubbed her shoulder and drew her closer. "You've got to stop thinking about it."

Maybe in his world that was how you learned to deal with things. You acted when needed and then you stopped thinking about it. But as she met Matt's caring hazel gaze, it was clear he was thinking about it. About her and all that had happened.

She offered him a tender smile and cupped his jaw. *"Gracias."*

His brow furrowed and his gaze narrowed in puzzlement. "For what?"

"For understanding. For having my back."

"Always. I'll always have your back," Matt said, and with those words, relief swamped her, and when he pulled her closer, she nestled into his side.

SABOTAGE OPERATION

New York Times Bestselling Author

CARIDAD PIÑEIRO

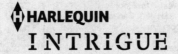

HARLEQUIN

INTRIGUE

To my daughter Samantha Ann

So proud of you and all that you've accomplished with
Seoul Searching and all your other books!

ISBN-13: 978-1-335-59166-1

Sabotage Operation

Copyright © 2024 by Caridad Piñeiro Scordato

Recycling programs
for this product may
not exist in your area.

Harlequin Enterprises ULC
22 Adelaide St. West, 41st Floor
Toronto, Ontario M5H 4E3, Canada
www.Harlequin.com

Printed in Lithuania

MIX
Paper | Supporting
responsible forestry
FSC® C021394

USA TODAY bestselling author **Caridad Piñeiro** is a Jersey girl who just wants to write and is the author of nearly fifty novels and novellas. She loves romance novels, superheroes, TV and cooking. For more information on Caridad and her dark, sexy romantic suspense and paranormal romances, please visit www.caridad.com.

Books by Caridad Piñeiro

Harlequin Intrigue

South Beach Security: K-9 Division

Sabotage Operation

South Beach Security

Lost in Little Havana
Brickell Avenue Ambush
Biscayne Bay Breach

Cold Case Reopened
Trapping a Terrorist
Decoy Training

Visit the Author Profile page at Harlequin.com.

CAST OF CHARACTERS

Matt Perez—Marine Matt Perez once worked with the K-9 division to search out IEDs and other explosive devices. When Matt retired from the service, he patrolled the streets of South Beach with his K-9 partner, but now he's one of South Beach Security's new K-9 agents.

Teresa Rodriguez—Teresa Rodriguez had once been an Olympic equestrian but fell in love with horse racing and now owns her own successful racing stable. She is supposed to testify against a former trainer accused of doping horses when she finds herself and her stables under attack.

Ramon Gonzalez III (Trey)—Marine Trey Gonzalez once served Miami Beach as an undercover detective. Trey has since retired and is now the acting head of South Beach Security and is hoping to expand it with the addition of a K-9 division.

Mia Gonzalez—Trey's younger sister Mia runs a successful lifestyle and gossip blog and is invited to every important event in Miami. That lets Mia gather a lot of information about what is happening in Miami to help Trey with running SBS.

Josefina (Sophie) and Robert Whitaker Jr.—Trey's cousins Josefina and Robert are genius tech gurus who work at SBS and help the agency with their various investigations.

Chapter One

The frantic pounding on the thick wooden door echoed through the early morning silence of the ranch house, dragging Teresa Rodriguez from the bills that had forced her awake.

She rushed to the front door, her riding boots hammering against the wood floor, and jerked it open. Her stable hand Luis stood there wringing his hands, wide-eyed and pale as milk.

"You have to come. Frijoles is down," the young man said, turned and raced in the direction of the stables.

Teresa tore after him, fear chilling her gut. Frijoles was not only her best friend, he was also her top stallion. She had been counting on the stud fees from breeding him to pay off the last of her debts. Without him...

She sprinted across her driveway and the dew-damp grass next to the stables. Her feet skidded on the pavers surrounding the building as she rounded the corner to the stable entrance, raced to the stallion's stall and caught sight of her trainer kneeling in the straw by her horse. The large bay's body twitched and convulsed beneath his hands.

"What happened, Richard?" she asked, squatting beside him. She joined the trainer in running her hands across the horse's muscled flanks to try to calm him as he thrashed his legs, rousing the straw's grassy smell.

The older man shrugged and dipped his head in the direction of her stable hand. "Luis said that Frijoles started acting up right after he began his morning feeding. When he went to check on him, the horse collapsed. That's when Luis got me. I've already called the vet. She's nearby and should be here soon."

"What can we do in the meantime?" she asked, her gut twisting into a knot as the horse's muscles shuddered beneath her palm. It pained her to see her horse hurting.

Richard tightened his lips and settled his hazel-eyed gaze on her. "I could give him some activated charcoal, but it could upset his gut."

"Do we know what caused this?" she asked and stroked the horse's side. His skin was slightly damp, and his powerful muscles shook violently. Choppy and irregular breathing, as if he couldn't catch his breath after a long race, had her breath trapping in her chest with fear.

"Maybe something he ate," Richard said with a shrug. "Let's check his feed bucket."

She looked over at the young stable hand who stood a few feet away, nervously twisting his hands. Worry and guilt were evident in his eyes, and she rose and laid a hand on his arm to calm him.

"It's nothing that you did, Luis. Can you show me Frijoles's feed for this morning?"

Luis nodded, walked to the corner of the stall where a large plastic feed bucket hung and came back with it.

Frijoles had only eaten part of his breakfast, and as she examined it, she noticed something unusual. Mixed in with the alfalfa, oats and other nutrients were odd bits of green. She stuck her hand into the feed, sifted through it and discovered larger pieces of what looked like leaves. Oval-shaped and dark green. Nothing she immediately recognized, but she knew one thing: they didn't belong in the stallion's feed.

She walked over with some of the leaves and held them out so the trainer could see them.

Richard's eyes widened in shock. "Where did you get those?"

"They were in Frijoles's feed bucket."

"Looks like belladonna leaves. They're poisonous and if I'm right, we can't wait for the vet. I'll go prep the charcoal." He leaped to his feet, raced out of the stall and toward the tack room, where they kept an assortment of supplies for tending to the horses.

The horse whinnied and tried to raise his head but failed and restlessly shifted his legs against the soft straw bedding on the floor again.

"*Tranquilo*, Frijoles. You'll be okay, *por favor*," she crooned, trying to calm the stallion so that he wouldn't injure himself.

The screech of tires heralded the arrival of the vet and barely a few minutes later, Dr. Miranda Ramirez raced into the stall carrying a large leather bag.

"How is he?" Miranda asked and knelt in the straw beside the horse.

"He ate belladonna," Teresa said and held out her hand to show the vet the leaves she had found in the feed. A second later, her trainer returned with a large bucket filled with the activated charcoal solution and long vinyl tubing.

"Definitely belladonna. Keep him calm," Miranda said while she took a blood sample.

"We'll confirm the poisoning with this and some stool samples," the vet said. She finished drawing the blood and reached for a vial of something in her bag. At Teresa's questioning look, she said, "Neostigmine. It'll counteract the atropine toxin."

Teresa kept her hands on the horse, stroking and crooning, trying to keep the horse still while Richard and Miranda worked together, feeding the tubing through the horse's nostril until it reached his stomach. Once the tube was in place, Richard pumped the activated charcoal through the tubing with a large syringe while Miranda set up an IV with fluids.

"We may have to hospitalize Frijoles if he doesn't respond to this," she said as she inserted the catheter for the IV in the horse's foreleg and wrapped a bandage around it to keep it in place. Then she prepped the fluid bag, connected the tubing into the catheter and laid the fluid bag on the horse's flank. "I'll get a drip stand in a second," Miranda said.

"Whatever it takes," Teresa replied. The bay was not only her top breeder, he was a combination best friend and therapist. Whenever she started wondering if opening the stables had made sense, Frijoles was there to listen or take her for a spin along the track to calm her doubts and worries.

Miranda laid a hand on her arm, her touch reassuring. "We'll make him better. Don't worry."

Teresa nodded and attempted a smile, but it was as brittle as the thin layer of ice protecting orange trees against a freeze. She laid her hands on the bay and softly murmured to him, trying to comfort him.

Long minutes became an even longer hour. Her back ached from kneeling over the horse, but she kept at it, as did Richard and Miranda, tending to the horse until the trembling eased and his breathing became more regular. The bay was even relatively calm as Richard withdrew the nasogastric tube.

"He's responding," Miranda said happily and leaned

back onto her haunches. "We'll need to keep giving him the IV fluids and monitor for any signs of gut issues or laminitis."

"*Gracias*, Miranda. Richard. You know Frijoles means the world to me," she said as they all came to their feet and wiped bits of straw from their pants legs.

"I have another call to make but will be back in about an hour to keep up the treatment," Miranda said, reaching for her medical bag. She shot another look at the horse and said, "Just keep him quiet and replace the IV bag when it's empty."

"I'll do that. Thanks again, Miranda," Richard said and held his hand out in the direction of the stall door. "I'll walk you to your car."

Teresa watched as Richard escorted the vet from the stall. She'd always thought her trainer had a thing for the beautiful vet. When Miranda offered him a shy smile, it seemed as if the feeling might be mutual. They made a good-looking couple.

Even at sixty, Richard was physically fit and imposing, with a thick thatch of salt-and-pepper hair, a strong jaw and sharp hazel eyes. Miranda was a decade younger, with coffee-brown hair just showing the first few strands of gray, chocolate brown eyes and an hourglass figure that would tempt most men.

Frijoles knickered as if complaining he didn't have her beside him, and Teresa kneeled next to him once more. "You're going to be fine," she murmured and stroked his flank.

The horse blew out a breath through his nostrils, almost in agreement, and closed his eyes, seemingly comfortable now that he had her attention.

Much like whoever had been playing the little tricks

around the stables now had her complete attention. She'd tried to write off all the other things as forgetfulness or accidents, but they had stressed her out. The unlocked gate at the paddock that had let some of the other horses roam into a neighboring avocado grove. The small electrical fire in the corner of a shed that housed spare tack. The waterlogged packages holding the new silks that her jockeys would wear in a few months when the racing season began.

She couldn't keep on ignoring those incidents anymore and she suspected who was behind all the mayhem: Warner Esquivel, her former trainer who was being investigated by the racing commission. She'd fired him years earlier because she'd caught him drugging one of her mares. Now the racing commission wanted her to testify against Esquivel.

It was painfully obvious that she had underestimated what he would do to keep her quiet. Luckily, she knew what to do to protect herself, her people and her horses.

Pulling her cell phone from her jeans pocket, she dialed her friend Mia Gonzalez. Mia's family ran South Beach Security and she trusted that they could get to the bottom of whatever was happening.

Mia answered on the first ring. "*Hola, amiga*. It's so good to hear from you."

"I wish I could say this was a friendly call, but I need your help. Actually, I need SBS's help."

"Whatever you need," Mia said without hesitation.

Teresa breathed a sigh of relief, the first one since rushing to Frijoles's stall hours earlier. She hoped that with the Gonzalez family on her side, she could stop whoever was trying to hurt her and her business.

EVEN AFTER SIX months on the job it struck Matt Perez as odd to see his old friend Trey Gonzalez sitting behind a desk. Trey had always been an all-action guy from their time together in the Marines to their assignments on the Miami Beach police force.

But the desk job seemed to be working for Trey. Matt had never seen his friend looking happier, especially since his wedding a month earlier to Roni Lopez, who was still a detective with Miami Beach PD.

Although Trey's door was open, his head was buried in the papers on his desk, so Matt rapped his knuckles on the door to announce his arrival. Beside him his K-9 partner Butter bumped up against his leg and looked up at him, as if wondering what they were doing in the office. For the last six months they'd been spending time between an assortment of security jobs as well as training Butter on a variety of tasks. So far, the Belgian Malinois had been learning quickly and Matt hoped that in time, their working together would be as seamless as it had been with the K-9 partner he'd had while on the force.

"Come in, Matt," Trey called out and rose from the large glass-and-metal desk. He bro-hugged his old friend and bent toward Butter, but hesitated. "Is it okay to pet her?"

Normally he didn't permit people to treat his working K-9s as if they were domesticated companions, but Trey was the boss of his family's agency. As a K-9 officer for South Beach Security, Butter might have to one day interact with Trey, so it was good for her to be familiar with the other man.

"Sure. She should get to know you," Matt said and stood there holding the leash while Trey held his hand out for the dog to sniff.

Butter did that, but then hesitated and looked up at Matt, as if seeking his permission. With a smile, Matt said, "Good girl, Butter. This is Trey."

The dog finally sniffed Trey's hand, and sensing he was a friend and not a foe, the shepherd bumped her head against Trey's hand.

"You are a good girl," Trey said and knelt to rub the dog's head. Butter's tongue lolled out of her mouth with pleasure. Looking up at Matt, his friend said, "I gather her training is going well?"

Matt nodded. "It is. She's got a great sense of smell and handles instructions well. We're still learning a few things, but she's going to be a great K-9 partner."

"That's good to hear, because we've got an important case for you," Trey said and straightened. As he did so, his gaze drifted over Matt's shoulder toward the door.

Matt turned to find Trey's baby sister, Mia, standing at the door, beautiful as ever. She looked well considering she'd almost died after being shot two months earlier during a case that had threatened her newlywed husband as well as the Gonzalez family.

She was dressed casually today in jeans and a loose, pale pink tunic top. It made her look younger, especially since he was used to seeing her all done up in the designer clothes and shoes she wore when doing one of her social media gigs with her cousin Carolina. The two women, affectionately called "the Twins," had been familiar fixtures when he'd patrolled the South Beach scene with his K-9 partner.

Trey walked over to hug her and said, "Good morning, *hermanita*. How are you feeling?"

"Stronger every day," Mia said and then sashayed to his side and embraced him. "Good to see you, Matt."

"You, too, Mia. How are you adjusting to married life and working with Trey?" he asked, aware that the family members had faced serious challenges in recent months.

"I'm doing well but Carolina is missing me. I'm sure

she'd love some company," Mia said with a warm smile and a playful wink.

Even though Carolina was as smart and beautiful as Mia, Matt waved his hands in the air to dismiss any suggestion that he'd be interested in Carolina. "You rich girls are out of my league," he said and truly meant it. He'd been burned once by that kind of woman and had no desire to repeat the experience.

Trey clapped him on the back. "Let's get to it, then, although you may not like the assignment we're about to give you."

"Why's that?" Matt asked as he sat in front of Trey's desk and instructed Butter to lie down with a hand command. After, he rewarded his new partner with a "good girl" and the ear rubs she loved so well.

"Rich girl," Mia said with a laugh and sat in the chair next to him. "She's a very good friend who's working hard to get her business going and needs our help."

With a nod, Matt said, "Understood. What do you need me to do?"

Chapter Two

Teresa curled up close to Frijoles's flank, reassured by the regular breathing and restful muscles beneath her. She and Richard had tag-teamed throughout the night, changing out the IV fluid bags to keep the bay hydrated. The vet had returned several times as well to do another flush of the horse's stomach with the activated charcoal. Miranda and Richard had just left to get breakfast after the long night of worry and work.

The sound of footsteps on the pavement outside her horse's stall snared her attention. The shadowed figure of a tall man suddenly filled the doorway. Fear raced through her at the unfamiliar silhouette until a nice-sized dog came to sit beside the man and a smaller, more familiar, figure also joined him.

She stroked her horse's side with a reassuring caress and scrambled to her feet, brushing away any straw bits from her clothing.

"Is this a good time?" Mia Gonzalez asked and walked to the stall's entrance, but the man remained behind her, silent and still in shadow.

Frijoles had been resting quietly and blessedly improving, so it was as good a time as any. "Sure, but I need to stay close by," she said and gestured to the bay.

"Got it," Mia said.

Teresa walked out of Frijoles's stall but positioned herself where she could keep an eye on the horse. She hugged her friend and then faced the man who had finally moved into view and joined Mia in the space outside the stall.

She didn't know what hit her at the sight of him. He was tall. Well over six feet with broad shoulders that seemed as if they could carry the weight of the world. Dressed in pressed khakis and a polo branded with the SBS logo, he still had that kind of ramrod straight posture and precision dress that screamed military. But it was his blue-eyed gaze that captured her attention and held it. There was intelligence there, and determination. Also, that indefinable something that said not to mess with him. She was glad he was on her side. Or at least she hoped he was, since she sensed animosity in his glance as well.

Close to his leg a large shepherd waited, his long pointy ears straight up at attention and his tongue hanging out. It was a beautiful dog with light brown, almost golden fur with darker brown-black markings.

The man brought a strong hand to his mouth and faked a cough, making Teresa realize that Mia had said something she hadn't heard.

"I'm so sorry. It's been a long night," she said with a wave of her hand in the direction of the stall.

"That explains it," the man mumbled beneath his breath, earning a sharp elbow from her friend Mia.

She was confused until a light breeze wafted through the stable and she smelled herself much as he must have. Bright color flooded her cheeks, but she tamped it down and lifted her chin a challenging inch. "I had to take care of my horse."

"Admirable. I imagine…" He paused as he read the horse's name by the door of the stall. "Frijoles must be a big investment for you," he said, a slight drawl in his words. Texas, she guessed.

Frijoles was more than just an investment, not that this man needed to know. Holding out her hand, she realized it was smudged with dirt from the long night of caring for her horse. Determined not to let him faze her, she wiped her palm on her jeans and stuck out her hand again, daring him to refuse.

"Teresa Ramirez. I own Redland Ranch," she said, but thought, *Well, me and the bank*.

He took her hand. His palm was calloused. Slightly rough. The sign of a man who used his hands for a living. Strong, even as she knew he was tempering his strength for the handshake.

"Matthew Perez, SBS K-9 Division," he said, and his deep voice resonated inside, awakening chords that hadn't played in a long time.

Teresa glanced at Mia, unfamiliar with that part of her friend's family business. "Is this division something new?"

Mia smiled and nodded. "Trey has been taking over for my father and thinks it's time to offer more services to our clients. Matt is our first K-9 agent but not our last. We think having him here on the grounds directing our security detail is the best way to protect you."

Teresa looked between her friend and Perez. "Here? As in full-time on the premises?"

"We think that's best, if you have the space," he said, a hint of something in his tone that said he wasn't necessarily comfortable with the idea but was reluctantly going along with SBS's plans.

She didn't really have the space. She only had a small bunkhouse where her stable hand Luis lived. Richard and the rest of the staff lived off-site. As for her own home, there were three bedrooms, but having him there…

Glancing at him, it hit her that he'd be dangerous for her. There was something indefinable that called to her. Maybe it was the fact that she'd barely dated because she'd been too busy building the stables. No matter the reason, it would be hard having him around, but she'd put up with him to protect her horses.

Facing Mia, she reluctantly said, "I have a guest room at the ranch house."

It DIDN'T TAKE a genius to see that Ms. Ramirez wasn't in love with the idea of sharing a space with him and he got it. There was a rich girl buried beneath the grungy jeans, dirt-stained T-shirt and disheveled hair. He'd pulled up pictures of her on his smartphone while Mia and he had done the short drive from the SBS offices in downtown Miami to the Redland area where the stables were located.

A woman like *her* wouldn't want a man like *him* in her space.

"I can bunk down in here. Maybe a cot in the tack room?" It would be uncomfortable, but better than him having to put on airs around her.

With a slash of an elegant dirt-stained hand, Teresa said, "There's no way you'd be comfortable and that wouldn't be fair, especially since I've asked for your help."

"Maybe we can bring in an RV and park it near the ranch house? Does that sound acceptable?" Mia said, obviously sensing the tension between the two.

In the time he'd been with SBS, Matt had seen how Mia managed to be the mediator and problem solver, which was maybe how she'd built her own fortune as a social media influencer before joining her family's agency. Clearly, she could read people well.

"That's a great idea. We even have a power station and water hookup to the side of the house that the RV can connect to. We sometimes use it for visitors who bring their own lodging," Teresa said, the earlier tightness of her body flowing away with Mia's solution.

"Wonderful. I'll call Trey. We can probably get one here by later today. In the meantime, would you mind taking Matt around to show him the property? That'll give him an idea of what other security measures we'll need," Mia said and then faced Matt. "I'll head back to the office to wait for your report."

"I'll get it to you as soon as I can," Matt said, and with that, Mia headed out of the stables, leaving him and Butter alone with their new client.

"Would you like to get cleaned up first?" he asked and eyeballed her. A mistake. It was impossible to miss the beautiful woman beneath the grime and horse smell. A heart-shaped face was framed by loose, sun-streaked light brown hair that just skimmed her fine-boned shoulders. Eyes as green and hard as emeralds met his gaze.

She tilted that dimpled chin upward and looked down her perfectly perky nose, appearing decidedly too royal as she did so. It was a good reminder that she was way out of his league. "I'm fine just the way I am."

"Great. Then let's get going, and while we're at it, you can tell me more about what's been happening on the property," he said and clapped his hands, impatient to get going.

"Let me get Luis to come and stay with Frijoles," she said. She stepped away for a moment to make the call and returned, gesturing toward the entrance to the stables. As they walked down the space, she explained the area to him.

"These are the main stables. We have ten horses in here as well as a tack room where we keep saddles and other equipment."

One of the horses stuck its head out as they passed the stall, and Teresa stopped to stroke its nose. He paused as well, and Butter sniffed around the door to the stable before sitting at his side.

"This is Ay Caramba. She's one of my brood mares and expecting a foal any day now."

Matt nodded and watched as the horse knickered and tossed her head, as if wanting more of Teresa's attention. Teresa smiled and rubbed the horse's head. "No treats today, *chiquitica*."

"I guess no one messed with her feed?" Matt asked as Teresa moved away from the mare and headed toward the tack room in the stables.

"We checked all the other feed buckets. Only Frijoles's was poisoned," Teresa explained.

"Why Frijoles?" he asked, aware the horse was a winner from his brief research on the way over but needing to hear more from Teresa.

"He's my best stallion and…" She hesitated, clearly uncomfortable with revealing too much. When she failed to continue, he left it at that for the moment.

"Whoever did this knows he's important to the stable," Matt said to end the awkward silence caused by her reluctance.

Teresa nodded. "Yes, they know. They also seem to know how we work around here. They've done several things on the property without us seeing them."

"Like what?" He followed her into the tack room filled with an assortment of saddles and other equipment. At the far end of the room was another smaller room where he could see brightly colored uniforms hanging.

Teresa walked to the door of that room and gestured to the uniforms. "These are the new silks I ordered for this year's racing season."

"Silks?" he asked, confused by the reference.

"The uniforms. They're called silks because they used to be made out of silk. They're not anymore, luckily for us, because the box that the delivery person left at the ranch house door got soaked. We thought it was the sprinkler system at first, but then realized it hadn't been on when the damage occurred."

If someone knew that the box had been placed there, they had to either be watching somehow or a regular on the ranch. "Could you get me a list of people who work for you?" he asked.

She jerked back as if struck and raised a hand to her chest, clearly surprised by the request. "You think one of *my people* might possibly be doing this?"

"Anything is possible," he said, aware of that after his many years in the military and on the police force. Sometimes the people you trusted most were the ones you shouldn't have trusted.

"You're barking up the wrong tree," she said, hurrying out of the tack room and stables.

"What would be the right tree?" he asked, chasing after her with Butter until they reached a utility ATV sitting just outside the stables.

As she climbed into the driver's seat, she said, "Warner Esquivel. He was a trainer who worked for me and who's being investigated by the racing commission. I'm supposed to testify against him in a little over a week."

Matt considered her statement and was unconvinced but

remained silent. He commanded Butter up into the storage box behind the two seats of the ATV and rubbed her head to reward his K-9 partner. Slipping into the passenger seat, he asked, "Where to?"

Teresa waved her arm in the direction of the large open spaces beyond the stables. "The pastures and paddocks. That's where the first problems happened."

She whipped down the paved track that ran the length of the stable building and onto a dirt path that wound through her property. The ATV bounced and rocked from side to side as Teresa steered along the edges of the fenced paddocks. She gestured with her hand to the area. "About a month ago, one of the paddock gates was left open and a few of our horses wandered into a neighboring avocado grove. At first, we thought there was a problem with the gate latch, but it was fine."

"Could someone have accidentally left it open?" he asked and grabbed hold of the door frame as the ATV rocked violently over some uneven ground.

She shrugged, and seemingly unfazed by the roughness of the ride, said, "That's what we thought. So we didn't worry, but then it happened again a few days later and that time one of the horses almost got hit by a truck in the grove."

The ATV slowed toward the end of the paddock and turned onto a narrow path that ran along a small stand of trees. She stopped the vehicle and pointed to one of the paddocks. "That's one of our better grazing areas. But about a week after the horses got free, a break in the irrigation system flooded the area."

"I assume the break wasn't an accident," he said with an arch of his brow.

"Not an accident. Someone used a shovel to make cuts along the irrigation line." Teresa drove the ATV down the edge of the property, which was quite large. She handled the ATV capably along the slightly rough path, the dirt on her hands incongruous against the very feminine pink polish on her nails.

"How much land do you have here?" Matt asked, taking in the large open spaces surrounded by the nearby avocado grove and the long strip of woods along one edge of the property.

"A little over twenty acres. We need about an acre per horse to have the right amount of land for grazing and exercise. To the other side of the stables, we have a track where we train and that takes a lot of space," she explained.

Matt let out a low whistle. "And I imagine it must take a lot of money for upkeep on that much property."

TERESA GOT THE sense that having money was a problem with him, so she decided to set the record straight.

"It takes a lot of hard *work*, Mr. Perez," she said, anger sharpening her tone as she drove away from the woods and back toward the stables.

"Matt, please. I'm not that formal," he said. It tempered her anger, but only slightly as he said, "No insult intended, but I imagine that with Frijoles winning as many races as he has—"

"The purses are not as large as you might think. Plus, horses are expensive to keep. It's not just the land," she said and gestured to the area around them as she parked the ATV on the path by the stables. She faced him. "There are expenses for the vets, farriers—"

"Farriers?" Matt asked, a puzzled look on his face.

"The person who shoes the horses and takes care of their hoofs. I thought a Texas boy like you might have ridden a horse in his day," she challenged.

A bright flush worked across his cheeks and with a wag of his head, he said, "A lot of hard work and money, but I imagine your parents are a big help."

Anger rose up again, making her wonder if it made sense to have this man around 24/7. "My family and their money have nothing to do with *my* business. I succeed or fail on my own," she said and hopped out of the ATV.

Matt slipped from the ATV and motioned for Butter to join him. As the dog came to his side, a bright flash of light from the woods across from the stable warned him to act.

He grabbed Teresa around the waist and hauled her into the stables just as a bullet slammed into the wood of Ay Caramba's stall.

The brood mare nervously danced away, and Butter fought against her leash, aware of the danger, as another bullet nicked the door frame to the stable.

"Is there another way out?" he asked as the gunfire continued, spooking the horses as bullet after bullet peppered the brick building and the nearby stall.

She motioned to the far end of the stables. "We can open the other door."

He shoved a finger in her face and warned, "You stay here."

With a softly worded command to Butter, he and the shepherd raced to the far end of the stables. He carefully opened the large door made of wood and wrought iron, uncertain whether there was a second attacker who might fire from a different angle. The only gunfire was from the other end of the stable, so he rushed out, trying to keep out of sight of the shooter in the woods.

He worked his way to the edge of the building and once

again caught sight of the flash of light, probably the sun-light reflecting off the rifle's scope.

If he'd had his old K-9 partner, he might have moved closer and sicced the dog on their assailant, but Butter was still a novice, and the attack command was relatively new to her. Plus, it was a long dash from the stables to any kind of cover.

But as another burst of gunfire slammed into the build-ing, and the sounds of the frightened horses and Teresa trying to calm them registered, Matt had no choice but to risk it.

Chapter Three

Teresa's heart beat a staccato rhythm in her chest as the rain of bullets struck the brick of the building and the wood of Ay Caramba's stall. Her mare circled the stall, eyes wild with fear, while the horses in the nearby stalls responded, prancing and pacing in their stalls and voicing complaints in a chorus of nickers, huffs and whinnies.

She worried the mare might hurt herself and her baby but couldn't risk going in through the stall door as another bullet bit into the wood. She would be too exposed to the shooter if she went in that way.

But as another scared whinny came from inside Ay Caramba's stall, she had to do something.

She raced into Frijoles's stall, where an equally frightened Luis kneeled by the bay, trying to keep him calm.

"Give me a leg up," she said and motioned toward the wall between the stalls.

Luis was immediately at her side and offered his clasped hands as a way to boost her up. She grabbed the top of the wall and went up and over into the neighboring stall, where the mare was prancing nervously. Hurrying to the mare's side, she slipped an arm around her neck and stroked her hand down the horse's bulging belly, trying to calm her and move her out of sight of the shooter. Avoiding hooves that could crush a foot or worse if they landed on her.

As the sound of gunfire shifted away from the stables, the horse calmed but Teresa's fear remained with the thought of what Matt might be doing to draw the shooter away from them and to himself.

MATT MANAGED TO make it around the back of the stables and to the track area, where he found another ATV. He commanded Butter into the passenger seat beside him so he could protect her from the gunfire.

Speeding along a path toward the woods, he kept the paddock fencing as a barrier between him and the shooter. A bullet bit into the wooden fencing and ricocheted against the bumper of the ATV. A second one whizzed by his head, making him crouch lower to lessen the mass he presented to their assailant.

At the end of the path, he jerked the ATV to a stop and called out to Butter, "Come here, girl." Together they raced into the woods for cover.

Gunfire peppered the trees in front of them, sending bits of bark and leaves flying all around them, but Matt and Butter stayed low, avoiding the bullets. He reached into the holster tucked against the small of his back and withdrew the HK 9mm he kept there. Slowly he moved toward the shooter's position, keeping Butter close to his side. She hadn't had much attack training yet, but he hoped she would respond when commanded.

Not that hope was a plan.

He pressed forward and the shooter sprayed their area with gunfire again, but it was the kind of blind shooting that said their assailant didn't have their precise position. Reassured by that, he tried to move as silently as he could with his K-9 partner, almost crawling in the direction where he'd seen the flash of the rifle scope and heard the gunfire.

He guesstimated that he was no more than fifty yards from the shooter, but as he searched the area, there was no sign of anyone in the woods and the gunfire had stopped. The underbrush was thick, though, and provided good cover. He wasn't sure if the shooter had escaped.

Muttering a curse under his breath, he hurried forward until he noticed an area with trampled vegetation underfoot. He examined the ground and noticed a few brass casings from a rifle. A .224 caliber bullet for sure. Unfortunately, a common caliber for many popular rifles. That could be why the shooter had left the brass behind. Either that or he was an amateur who didn't know to police his brass.

"Come here, Butter. Find it," he said, motioning the dog into the flattened underbrush.

Butter sniffed around and began to paw the ground, letting him know she'd found a scent. At another "Find it" command, Butter took off and Matt followed, noticing the disturbances along the ground that had created a path through the woods. The shooter hadn't been careful to hide his tracks, maybe because of his haste to escape.

While Matt moved, he stayed alert to any threats, aware the perp might be waiting to take them out.

The far edge of the woods led to a grassy break between Teresa's property and the avocado grove. The shooter's footprints were visible along the ground, and he avoided them to preserve the crime scene. Barely yards ahead were clear tire tracks moving away from a spot where their assailant must have parked his vehicle.

Satisfied the attacker was gone and no longer a threat, he tucked his pistol back into its holster and whipped out the phone to call Trey. As his friend and boss answered, he said, "We're going to need more boots on the ground ASAP."

TERESA STOOD BY the entrance to the stables, arms across her chest as she tried to keep herself calm while an assortment of police officers and SBS personnel swarmed around her property.

In the stable area, one of the CSI members searched the area for remnants of the bullets while in the far woods another team worked the stand of trees.

Matt stood beside Mia and her tech guru cousins Sophie and Robbie. She had met the cousins more than once during visits to the Gonzalez family home and the recent dual wedding for Trey and Roni, and Mia and John Wilson, a multimillionaire tech genius who sometimes assisted the family with their investigations.

Matt looked in her direction and as their gazes met, she detected the worry in his expression but also compassion. With a wave of his hand, he invited her to join them, and she ambled over, stood between Mia and him as he explained what he wanted.

"I think we need to get some trail cams and security guards along the edges of the property as well as security cameras in and around the stables. Also, some cameras on the ranch house," he said, gesturing to the various areas with a sweep of his muscled arm.

"We can get some of that done today. I assume you want to be able to monitor the feeds?" Sophie said and Matt nodded.

Robbie looked back to where the SBS team had brought an RV and parked it beside the ranch house. "We'll have to make sure you have a clean internet connection in that RV to pick up the feeds."

"And enough power and room for all the monitors," Sophie said. It was impossible to miss the concern and doubt in her voice.

"You can have all that in the ranch house," Teresa said in a shaky voice, nervous about having Matt's presence in her safe space. But it was what made the most sense considering what had happened barely an hour earlier.

Mia picked up on her emotions immediately. "Are you sure? We can make the RV work."

Teresa glanced from the RV to her house and appreciated the effort that Mia and SBS had already made, but the most important thing was putting an end to the danger.

"I'm sure. Whatever you need to do, only…" She hesitated as her mind raced with worry about not only how his presence would affect her, but also about how much this was all going to cost. She was barely making ends meet, and with this…

"We take care of our friends," Mia said and laid a comforting hand on her arm, silently understanding Teresa's concerns.

Teresa forced a smile. "*Gracias*, but I don't expect you to do this for free."

Mia nodded, as did Sophie and Robbie. "It won't be free, but we won't break the bank either. We know how hard you're working to build this place."

"I appreciate that. Whatever you need, just let me know," she said, and they were about to resume their discussion when Luis ran up to them.

"*Señorita* Teresa. You have to come see," he said, a broad smile on his young face.

They followed him to Frijoles's stall, where the large bay was on his feet.

Teresa's throat choked with emotion, making it almost impossible to breathe. Happy tears spilled down her face. Overwhelmed with relief, she turned, and Matt was there, his blue-eyed gaze understanding, drawing her in.

MATT COULD HANDLE a lot of things but not a woman's tears. Especially as his eyes met Teresa's and observed her immense love for the animal standing behind her in the stall. Love and relief. They pulled at his heart in a way that he hadn't experienced in far too long.

But she suddenly covered her face, stepped toward him and almost melted against his chest.

Surprised, he hesitated, unsure of what to do, but instinct took over and he awkwardly wrapped his arms around her to offer support as she cried out her emotions. He couldn't remember the last time he'd offered comfort, and it had been even longer since he'd received it.

"It's going to be okay," Matt said, and Teresa nodded against his chest.

"It is," she murmured and took a step back. She wiped the tears from her face, glanced up at him and said, *"Gracias."*

He didn't feel as if there was all that much for her to be thanking him for but nodded anyway. "We should get to work on securing this place."

"Yes, of course," Teresa said and turned to Mia, Sophie and Robbie. "I shouldn't keep you from doing your work."

Mia laid a reassuring hand on her arm again and gave her an understanding smile. "It's been a rough twenty-four hours. Why don't the two of us go back to the ranch house so you can get some rest while Matt, Sophie and Robbie deal with the police."

"That's a good idea. It'll give me a chance to get cleaned up as well," Teresa said. She ran a hand through her tangled hair and glanced at her dirty clothes.

The two women walked off in the direction of the ranch house, their heads tucked close as they chatted along the way.

Matt watched, drawn to Teresa's quiet strength and her beauty. It would be hard to ignore the beauty even as her strength threatened to pull him in. He'd always admired that in a woman, but he reminded himself that he was here to do a job and that Teresa was the kind of woman to avoid.

Facing Sophie and Robbie, he went over the areas in the stables where he thought they needed cameras. Then the trio walked outside, and he once again suggested possible locations for cameras and discussed the protection for the perimeter of the property.

"Teresa told me they've had incidents at various spots in the paddocks. Up until today, mostly nuisance kind of things. We need eyes on the ranch but it's over twenty acres and I can't imagine fencing all that in."

Sophie peered around the property. "You had a good idea about the trail cameras around the perimeter. It's such a large property that security guards alone can't keep it safe."

"I agree, but I plan on taking Butter around as well to keep an eye on the place," Matt clarified.

"A lot of ground to cover but we can put cameras on that paddock fencing as well to keep an eye on who's coming and going," Robbie said as he gazed over the property.

"Lights will help. Some motion sensor floods along the edges of the wooded area and by the stables and ranch house might be good," Matt suggested.

"Solar-powered will make them easier to install and we can get ones with wireless cameras built in," Sophie said.

Matt nodded. "That makes a lot of sense. Do you think you can get that done today? It's late already."

Sophie and Robbie shared a look. With a shrug, Robbie said, "It's a lot to do but if we bring in a few more of our techs, we can secure the house and stables today and finish up the perimeter by tomorrow."

"That's acceptable. We'll place a few guards along the perimeter. Butter and I will patrol the grounds tonight.

Right, Butter?" Matt rubbed the dog's head as she calmly sat beside him, patiently waiting for his instructions.

"We'll get to work, then," Sophie said, and she and Robbie walked away, but just as they did so one of the police officers who had been investigating the shooting approached him.

"Officer Perez," she said, recognizing him from his time on the police force. She was one of the younger officers and he remembered when she'd first come out of the academy. She'd been eager and easygoing, and from what he'd seen of her today, her time on the force hadn't yet dimmed her enthusiasm for the job.

He dipped his head in greeting. "Officer Ventura. It's just Matt now," he said with a broad smile.

"Matt," she acknowledged with a nod and opened her notepad. "Thanks for preserving the crime scene. The CSI officers have been able to collect several brass casings and bullets as well as casts of the footprints and tire tracks. Can you supply any details about the shooter?"

Matt shook his head. "When he first started shooting, I was too far away, and he was hidden in the woods. By the time I got closer, he'd escaped but Butter was able to pick up a scent."

"You keep on saying *he*," the young officer challenged.

"I only had a quick look at the footprints but based on the size and their depth in the softer ground, it was probably a man. Too big and heavy for a woman," he explained.

Officer Ventura nodded, pen poised over the notepad. "Anything else you can report?"

With another shake of his head, he said, "Nothing. SBS will be securing the property but anything you find out will be appreciated."

"We'll keep you advised of developments and hope

you'll do the same," the officer said, closed her notepad and tucked it into a holder on her duty belt.

"We will, Officer Ventura," he replied with an easy smile.

"Vanessa, please, Matt," she said with a sexy grin and walked away with a decidedly enticing sway despite the heavy leather belt cinched around her hips.

It took him a moment to realize she'd been flirting with him. He'd clearly been out of the game for way too long not to notice, but then again, he'd been focused on his career since joining the military at eighteen and the police force years later. His few relationships hadn't lasted long, and meaningless hookups had never been his thing.

For some reason, a vision of kissing Teresa Ramirez blasted into his brain. Driving away the unwanted temptation, he surveyed the area to find Sophie, Robbie and two of the SBS installers hard at work by the stables. He decided it was time to give Mia a report and see how Teresa was doing.

"Come, Butter," he commanded softly, and the shepherd padded beside him to the door of the ranch house.

Teresa's home was a simple but welcoming two-story farmhouse with a large, screened front porch that faced the circular driveway and a small pond. Fat cattails surrounded the pond at one end while colorful water lilies floated toward the front. A water feature in the center of the pond gently sprayed water that cascaded down to dance on the surface. A flash of gold and white hinted at the fish beneath the surface. He could picture sitting on the porch to watch the sunset and keep an eye on the nearby stables.

He paused at the door to the house, worried about what awaited him inside. Teresa had clearly experienced a roller coaster of emotions today, from worry at what had been happening to fear with the shooting and finally relief that her stallion was feeling better. He hoped that she'd be calmer and free of the tears that had tugged at his heart earlier. Those tears had opened a crack in his heart that he had to seal right back up if he was going to do this job properly.

Sucking in a breath, he knocked and waited to enter.

Chapter Four

The shower had done her a world of good. Besides removing the stink and dirt from the night spent caring for Frijoles, it had helped wash away some of the fear. Especially now that SBS was here and taking steps to protect her and her business. It had also helped wash away the memories of what it felt like to be pressed against Matt's hard chest and the way his arms had wrapped around her. Hesitantly, almost clumsily at first, before he fully committed to comforting her.

He clearly wasn't used to such things, which made her wonder about him. Wonder what had shaped the man who had promised to keep her safe.

Shaking away those thoughts, she finished drawing a brush through her hair and headed out to the living room, skipping a blow-dry since she wanted to be able to take part in whatever SBS was planning.

As she stepped into the living room, Mia was just letting Matt into the house.

It was unnerving having him in her home. She didn't know why, but there was something about the K-9 agent that demanded her attention. When he walked in, he glanced in her direction and met her gaze.

Was there relief there and maybe something else? she wondered.

"You're feeling better," he said, and it wasn't a question.

She nodded. "I am."

Mia looked from her to Matt, her gaze questioning. "Everything okay?"

Matt nodded. "They're installing the cameras by the stables and should be able to do the ones in and around the ranch house by tonight. In the meantime, I'll do perimeter checks this evening as well as keep an eye on the camera feeds."

Mia asked Teresa, "Where would you like us to set up the monitors for the security cameras?"

Teresa gestured to the far side of the living room. "The formal dining room makes sense. I hardly ever use it."

"Great. Trey should be here any minute now. He's bringing the equipment, techs and dinner. Roni may be joining us as well to let us know what the police have been able to get so far in their investigations," Mia said, walked to the door of the dining room and nodded, confirming the space would be okay.

Dinner? Teresa took a quick look at her watch. It was just past six but with everything that had been happening she'd lost track of time.

"We can eat at the kitchen table. Can I get you anything while we wait for Trey?" Teresa said.

"I'm good. What about you, Matt?" Mia asked.

"Water would be good. Thanks," he said, and she was about to guide them into the kitchen when a knock came at the front door.

"Come in," Teresa called out and Trey hurried in, a large box in his hands. Behind him on the walk leading to the house were two women wearing SBS polo shirts and hauling a small cart loaded with equipment.

Trey slipped the box to one hand and came over to embrace her, one strong arm wrapping around her waist. "How are you doing?" he asked, his tone one of brotherly concern.

With a hesitant shrug, she said, "As well as can be expected."

"Where can I put dinner and the equipment?" he asked.

"Dinner is in the kitchen and everything else can go in the dining room. I think you know the way," she said because both Trey and Mia had been at her house several times over the years.

Trey walked back to Matt and handed him the box. "Do you mind helping Mia and Teresa get set up for dinner?"

"Whatever you need, Trey," he said and looked in her direction. "Lead the way."

She smiled, gestured toward a door at the back of the living room and walked there, Mia, Matt and Butter following her into a large, open-concept room that held the kitchen, informal living room and a big-sized, farmhouse-style table for eating.

Matt placed the box on a counter and with a flip of a hand in the direction of the sink, he said, "Mind if I clean up?"

"Make yourself at home," she said, especially since he would be making her home his home during his security detail.

He went to the sink, Butter at his side. While he washed up, soaping his hands and forearms, the dog waited at his side patiently.

"Can I get anything for your dog?" she asked.

"A bowl would be nice so she can get a drink. I have her food and other things in Mia's car and can get those later," he said, turned from the sink and whipped some paper towels off a holder to dry his muscled forearms.

While she went to get the bowl, Mia finished emptying

the box onto the counter, and as she did so, the enticing aroma of citrus-marinated pork wafted into the air. Teresa's stomach growled, anticipating what she hoped would be Cuban sandwiches chock-full of roast pork, Swiss cheese and sweet ham. Grabbing a large mixing bowl, she filled it with water and set it on the floor by the end of the counter for Matt's dog.

Matt unleashed Butter and gave her a hand command. The shepherd headed to the bowl and lapped up some water before settling down on the floor, her large head nestled on her paws.

In an efficient ballet, Teresa took out plates, cutlery and napkins that Matt and Mia laid out on the table. It wasn't long before Trey walked in, Sophie and Robbie behind him. His phone dinged. He looked at it and said, "Roni says she'll be here in five minutes."

"I'm looking forward to hearing what she has to say," Mia said as she finished setting the table.

"Hopefully the police will have more info," Trey added and removed some other dishes from the box he had brought. "What can you tell us, Matt?"

Teresa walked over and took the takeout dishes to the table while Matt relayed what had happened earlier that day as well as the other incidents that had led to her calling Mia.

"Did you call him Frijoles because of his color?" Trey asked, brows furrowed as he puzzled about the name.

Teresa smiled and nodded. "I did. He's a black bay, so he's actually dark brown with a black tint to his skin and black points."

At Trey's slightly confused look, she explained, "His points—legs, ears and mane—are all black."

"He's a good-looking horse. Is it true you got him in a claiming race?" Matt said as he finished setting the table.

"He caught my eye in another race. Richard liked him as well. Thought he had untapped potential. Turns out Frijoles's father won over $2.3 million in purses, and we decided to put in a claim. He cost me $30,000 but he's been worth every penny," Teresa said, pride filling her voice.

A knock came at the door and Trey walked out to answer. He returned a second later with Roni. As he wrapped his arm around Roni's waist, Teresa noticed the baby belly bump that hadn't been visible at their wedding a month earlier.

Walking over, she hugged the other woman and said, "Welcome and congratulations. When are you due?"

"Another six months," Roni said with a grin and hugged her back.

"Will you keep working all that time?" Being an undercover Miami Beach detective wasn't the easiest of jobs.

Roni and Trey shared a look before Roni shrugged and said, "We've been talking about me joining SBS."

That prompted a big shout from Robbie and hugs from Mia and Sophie.

"That'll make it all of the family," Mia said with a joyful laugh.

"Well, except for Pepe, but you know how he is about SBS," Sophie said with a wry twist of her lips, reminding Teresa about the one Gonzalez cousin who wanted no part of the family business.

"I imagine Roni's tired, so why don't we get going on dinner," Mia said, ever the organizer and problem solver.

They settled around the large kitchen table, and she found herself sitting next to Matt whether by design or just plain bad luck. It was hard to ignore his presence between the size of him and his smell, something piney and clean despite the rough day they'd had.

A second later he handed her a plate with a Cuban sandwich, sweet *maduros*, rice and black beans, and she thanked him. Her appetite had been off since all the incidents had started but surrounded by the love and protection of the Gonzalez family and Matt, she was suddenly hungry.

She ate with gusto as the family started sharing the information they'd gathered so far, and it struck her how odd it was that they were mixing a family dinner and mayhem as if it was just any other day. But then again, maybe that was what made SBS so successful at what they did.

The bonds of family combined with brains and bravery made for an invincible mix.

MATT LISTENED INTENTLY as Roni ran down what the police had gathered so far.

"They have a partial on one of the casings, but it was smudged. They're not sure they'll be able to do anything with it," she said with a frown.

"What about the footprints and tire tracks?" he asked, impatient to hear more.

"Size ten sneaker. No ID yet on the brand. Off-road tires, a lug type typical of a four-by-four," Roni said.

"Common shoe size and tires," Matt said, worried that what the police had so far wouldn't help identify whoever wanted to hurt Teresa.

Trey nodded in agreement. "Too common and I assume there's no CCTV anywhere in the area," he said and took a bite of his sandwich.

"No CCTV. The area's too rural even though we're this close to Miami," Roni said and held her thumb and forefinger together to emphasize the small distance between the city and Redland.

"Poisoning Frijoles and the shooting are a big escalation of the other incidents," Matt cautioned and shot a look at Teresa. She had been eating heartily up until now, but with his words, she set down the sandwich and met his worried gaze.

Mia, who was sitting beside Teresa, laid a comforting hand on her arm. "Don't worry. We'll get to the bottom of this. Right, Matt?"

He didn't fail to hear the warning in Mia's tone to be gentler with her friend. "That's right and now that we're here, the stables and Teresa will be safe."

Despite his reassuring words, Teresa said, "Esquivel wants to make sure I don't testify."

"What's the worst they could do to him if you testify?" Trey asked around a mouthful of sandwich.

With a shrug, Teresa said, "A lifetime ban isn't likely for just drugging a horse or using a banned substance. Maybe a few months or more."

"People kill for less," Robbie said, earning a sharp elbow from his younger sister, Sophie, and a hushed *"cállate"* urging him to shut up.

People do kill for less, Matt thought. But there was something about today's incidents that rankled him, and as he looked across the table to Trey it was obvious his friend felt the same way. That was confirmed when Trey said, "What if it isn't Esquivel behind today's attacks?"

Chapter Five

Teresa almost jumped beside him. "What do you mean? Who else could it be? He's been calling and texting me about the hearing, but I haven't responded."

Trey shot him another look and then glanced at Mia, who seemingly understood where Trey was going.

"Your parents—" Mia began, but Teresa immediately cut her off.

"My parents have nothing to do with the stable. Nothing," Teresa said with an angry slash of her hand.

Matt knew only a little about Teresa's background, basically what Mia had told him on the way over: that her parents ran one of the larger casinos in the Miami area. From what little he knew of casinos and gambling, there was always the risk of criminal activity.

Not wanting to upset her because of Mia's earlier silent warning, he said, "We know your parents aren't involved with the stables, but is it possible—"

"They're not involved with the mob. I know people think that about casinos, but my parents are clean and always have been," she said with another sharp and emphatic slash of her hand.

"But what if the mob wants them to be?" Mia said cautiously and comforted Teresa once again with a gentle hand.

Matt soothed her as well, stroking her back with a fleeting caress.

She shot him a half glance and he couldn't fail to see the sheen of tears in her eyes. His heart did that strange little constriction again before he pulled away to glance at the Gonzalez family members seated at the table.

"We'll have the stables fully secured by tomorrow night. That may keep whoever it is away," he said and silently added *for a little while*.

With a sharp dip of his head, Trey said, "It will. In the meantime, we'll investigate Esquivel from our end and re-convene here tomorrow night to share what we've been able to gather."

Roni picked up her sandwich again and motioned with it. "Eat up. We're going to need the energy, especially you, Matt. You're going to do patrols with Butter tonight?"

Matt nodded. "I am and I'll keep an eye on the monitors as well."

"If you want, Sophie and I can tap into the feed and take turns monitoring so you can concentrate on the patrols and get some rest," Robbie offered.

Sophie nodded her head in agreement. "I had planned on staying up late to work on some other things anyway."

"*Gracias*. I'll take any help I can get," Matt said. He plucked some of the meat and cheese from his sandwich and clicked his tongue to call over Butter. When she approached, he fed her the food as a treat.

"I APPRECIATE ALL you're doing but is there anything else I can do to help?" Teresa said, wishing there was more she could do to stop the menace to her stables. Especially now that it was threatening innocent people and animals.

Matt, Luis and her horses could have been hurt today by the shooter. Richard and Miranda as well.

Trey hesitated and said, "Just keep an open mind about the investigation."

Teresa had no doubt what Trey wanted: for her to consider that something to do with her parents was causing the attacks. But she knew her parents and she knew they would never do anything illegal. Despite that, she said, "I'll try."

"That's all we ask," Mia said. Then they all turned their attention to finishing their meals with small talk about what they would each do and joking with Sophie and Robbie about how they would have to finally leave their computers to spend time in the countryside.

"You forget we've got our Whitaker family in Colorado. We're used to being out in the wild with them," Sophie said with a smile.

Teresa wasn't sure she'd call Redland the wilds of anything. Just over forty minutes from downtown Miami, it was a mostly agricultural area dotted with an assortment of fruit orchards, ornamental nurseries and some tourist attractions like Monkey Jungle and the Fruit and Spice Park.

"I've even been on a horse," Robbie said with a wry grin.

"It wasn't a pretty sight. I wasn't much better," Sophie added with a laugh.

"I have some saddle horses if you ever want to give it another try. Mia and I used to ride together when we were younger," Teresa offered and shot a quick look at her friend.

Mia chuckled and shook her head. "I managed to stay on, but you were amazing. You should show Matt your medals and trophies while he's here."

The heat of a blush erupted across her cheeks, especially as Matt turned that blue-eyed gaze in her direction. "You're a jockey? Aren't you too...tall for that?"

She shook her head. "I am too tall and heavy to be a jockey although I do train the horses. I did dressage."

"That's that fancy riding, isn't it?" he said with a low whistle.

"I figured him for a cowboy the first time we met and then he told me he was from Texas and confirmed it," Trey said, his tone that of a longtime friend.

"Not everyone from Texas is a cowboy. And I figured Trey for a spoiled rich boy what with his fancy clothes and haircut. I think he wanted to cry when they buzzed it all off," Matt teased back and mimicked someone running a razor across his head.

Trey dragged his fingers through the longer strands of his dark hair at the top of his fade cut. "Luckily it grows back."

Like it had for Matt, whose light brown hair was longer and with waves that emphasized his blue eyes, strong jaw and lips that… She wouldn't think about his lips. It was unwanted temptation to have thoughts about Matt she hadn't had in years thanks to the demands of building her racing stable.

"I guess you met in the Marines?" she asked, knowing that Trey had served before joining the police force and then his family's business.

Matt nodded. "We met in boot camp and then we were both stationed in Iraq. Trey was a grunt, and I was a dog handler."

Which explained to Teresa why Matt was now part of SBS's K-9 division. It also spoke to the loyalty between the two men that after their years of military and police service, they were working together again.

"And a good handler at that. Saved our butt from IEDs more than once. You can count on him, Teresa. Don't doubt that," Trey said with a jab of his finger in her direction to emphasize his words.

"I won't," she said and shot a half glance at Matt, who nodded to confirm his friend's statement.

"You *can* count on me," he echoed, reassuring her.

"Gracias," she said and smiled with gratitude.

With a loving look at his wife, Trey wrapped his arm around her shoulders and said, "I think it's time we got going. We've got a lot of work to do and I'm sure Roni's getting tired."

With a weary smile, Roni said, "I am a little beat, but I will reach out to the officers working this case."

Teresa suspected that as tired as Roni was, she'd be on the phone to her friends on the police force as soon as they left her property.

"We'll finish up what we can tonight and be back in the morning," Sophie said. Glancing at Robbie, she asked, "Do you want to do the last of the cameras or the monitors?"

"Monitors. The horses bring back too many painful memories," he said and chuckled.

"Once it's dark, I'll do my first patrol," Matt said, rising from the table. But as he did so, he grabbed his plate and said, "I'll help y'all clean up."

"Your mama raised you right," Teresa teased, appreciating that he hadn't assumed the womenfolk would do the cleaning.

He nodded, grinning. "My mama would be pleased by you saying that."

His drawl was decidedly more pronounced in this casual exchange, and she liked it maybe a little too much.

Mia also helped clean up while the rest of the crew finished installing the cameras and monitors. Matt went out to Mia's car to bring in his things as well as a dog bed, bowls and food for Butter, who had been patiently resting by the end of the counter. The dog quickly scarfed down the food, drank some water and then lay back down.

"She's such a good dog but who named her Butter?" Teresa asked as she looked at the Malinois.

Matt laughed. "Her breeder had a thing for the BTS K-pop band, so they named her for one of their biggest hits." Smiling, he knelt and rubbed Butter's long, pointy ears. "She is a good dog, and I should probably take her for a walk. Do you want to come with me?"

"Sure. Do you mind if I check in on the horses also?" she asked as she placed the last plate in the drying rack.

"Not at all," he said and together they strolled out of the ranch house and to the paved path to the stables, stopping to let Butter relieve herself. Matt cleaned up the mess into a poop bag that he left to pick up on the way back.

Once inside the stables, she went to Ay Caramba's stall and rubbed her hands along the mare's swollen flanks.

"You doing okay, *chiquitica*?" she crooned to the horse, who nickered and nipped at her shoulder. "Yes, I didn't forget," she teased and reached into her jeans pocket. She pulled out a sugar cube, placed it in the palm of her hand and the horse gently ate the treat.

"She likes her sweets," Matt said as he stood by the entrance to the stall and watched the exchange.

"She does, but they're not really good for her, so I keep them to a minimum." She walked out of the stall and secured the door.

When they reached Frijoles's stall, she was relieved to see the horse was standing and Luis was with him, holding up a feed bucket so Frijoles could eat. As she had done with Ay Caramba, she walked in and caressed the stallion's flanks, but he didn't budge from eating.

"I guess you're hungry, boy." She was happy to see he was feeling well enough to eat and so heartily also.

Matt stood at the stall door again, waiting, but Butter pawed at the ground near the entrance, impatient.

Matt spoke in easy tones to the dog. "Do you smell something, girl? Find it."

At his command the dog sniffed along the edges of the stall doors, moving to the far end of the building. Matt opened the large door to let the dog continue chasing the scent. Teresa followed behind them, wondering what scent the dog had found until Butter went directly to the shed where they had their spare tack room.

The dog pawed at the ground by the door and Matt glanced at her. "When was the last time you were in this shed?"

"Close to two weeks ago, when we emptied the tack after the small fire."

Matt nodded. "Please move back," he said with a pushing motion of his hand.

She did as he asked, shifting away from the door of the shed, and watched as he instructed Butter to sit. He dropped her leash and reached to the small of his back to withdraw his gun.

Her heart beat heavily in her chest as he grabbed the handle and released the latch to throw open the door, gun pointed into the shed.

After a sharp exhale, he said, "All clear."

Teresa released the breath she'd been holding and approached as he knelt by the door and gazed at the ground. "Someone's been in here."

Matt pointed to the ground, and she noticed half a dozen or so cigarette butts on the ground inside the shed.

"Did the fire start inside the shed? Maybe someone sneaking a smoke?" he asked.

Teresa shook her head. "No one on the ranch smokes and the fire was in that far corner by the electrical outlet. That's why we thought it was an accident, but then the other things happened, like the soaked silks."

"You didn't notice these butts?"

She shook her head again, more vehemently than before. "I'm sure they weren't there when we emptied the shed."

With a nod, Matt rose from his haunches and looked toward the house and stables. Raising his arm, he pointed in their direction. "From here he had a clear look at the house and stables. He'd know what was happening. When to do his attacks."

He reached into his jeans pocket and pulled out a plastic bag. Kneeling, he collected the butts, careful not to touch them. "I'll get these to the police so they can try to get some DNA off them. Maybe match it with a suspect in CODIS."

"CODIS?" she asked, unfamiliar with the term.

"Combined DNA Index System," he explained. "It's a database of DNA samples from criminal offenders. If whoever did this was arrested before, we'll get a hit."

"Will that take long?" she wondered aloud.

"Normally a few weeks but with Trey and Roni's pull, SBS might be able to get it done faster," he replied and held the bag up. "I need to call the PD to come and collect this."

"And what happens in the meantime?" she asked and followed him back toward the ranch house.

"We keep you safe."

Chapter Six

It was actually Trey and Roni who doubled back to pick up the evidence in order to drop it off with the detectives handling the case.

"Good job, Matt." Trey clapped him on the back.

"You mean 'good job, Butter.' She was the one who picked up the suspect's scent," Matt said, rubbing the shepherd's ears.

Trey smiled and patted the dog on the head. "Good job, Butter."

"We'll get this to the PD," Roni said as she took the evidence envelope from Matt.

"Thanks. It'll free me up to start the patrols now that it's dusk," he said and peered at the sky. By his guess, it would be dark within half an hour.

"We'll push them to do a rush on this," Roni said, and with that she and Trey left again.

Matt turned to Teresa. "You should go get some rest. It may take me a little while to patrol."

Teresa shot a hesitant look at the ranch house and then back at him. "I'm not really tired."

Despite what she said, he suspected it was more of an issue of her not wanting to be alone in the house with everything that was happening. He understood.

Jerking a thumb in the direction of the ATV by the stables, he said, "Want to come with me?"

"I'd like that," she said, her tone soft and grateful. It did something to his gut because he sensed she normally wasn't one to be indebted to anyone.

"You can tell me more about the stables while we patrol," he said as they slowly sauntered toward the ATV.

"I'm not sure there's much to tell," she said with a shrug.

Much as he had read her desire not to be alone earlier, he realized her reluctance to talk about the stables was more about humility than secrecy. Slipping into the ATV's driver's seat, he waited until she was settled on the passenger side and Butter was tucked into the storage box. He drove off in the direction of the track, an area he hadn't had a chance to explore before. Teresa had mentioned that it took up a great deal of the property and she hadn't been kidding. The track was a huge oval surrounded by the same kind of wooden split rail fencing that marked off the various paddocks on the other side of the property.

"What made you go from dressage to horse racing?" he said.

"I loved horses and couldn't imagine not being around them. I was boarding and training horses to pay for my dressage and realized that I loved the training part."

"And that led you to horse racing?" he asked and shot a quick look at her before he drove to the furthest part of the track, which was close to the street and visible to any passersby.

"An owner brought me a racehorse that was having a hard time getting into the starting gate. Someone recommended me since I'd trained one of their skittish animals. When I saw him race…it was magic. I got hooked on the idea of training my own racehorse."

He rounded the oval and caught sight of the guard whom Trey had placed at the perimeter of the property, close to the avocado grove and near the road.

The guard waved at them as they came around the bend and Matt turned to ride along the edges of the property.

"Is that when you bought this place?" he asked, his gaze skipping across the ranch. As big as the property was, he was more impressed by how everything seemed to be in tip-top shape.

"I had a smaller ranch I had managed to buy with some of the money I earned with an endorsement deal. I sold that one and financed the purchase of this one."

Although he hated to ask, he had to know. "Did your parents help with that?"

"No," she shot back quickly and with a sharp slash of her hand. "Like I told you all earlier, my parents have nothing to do with my stables."

He decided not to press the issue. At least not until he'd done more research on her parents and their business.

"What was this property before?" he asked, peering all around the grounds.

"It used to belong to an orchid grower who went out of business."

She gestured to the strand of trees that separated the ranch from the nearby groves. "Some of the orchids are native and you might be able to see them in those trees during the daytime."

Matt had been scanning the area as they drove, and he thought he'd noticed some flowers. "I'll look for them in the morning."

"I can point them out to you if you'd like," she said and grabbed hold of the frame of the ATV as they hit a bump that had them both rocking in their seats. Butter let out a little bark in seeming complaint as well.

"I'd like that, but first and foremost I have to focus on keeping you safe, Teresa." He shot her a look and said, "I plan on shadowing you around the ranch during the day if that's okay."

He waved at another guard situated at the deepest part of the property, near the spot where the shooter had hidden earlier that day.

"I'm okay with whatever you have to do," Teresa said but he could tell that she wasn't happy about the situation. He didn't blame her. Who could be happy about someone wanting to hurt you and your business?

They drove in silence until they reached the third guard positioned near the entrance to the ranch.

"Give me a second to check in with him," he said, stepped out of the ATV, and with a hand sign, commanded Butter to go with him.

TERESA WATCHED MATT as he ambled over to the armed guard. Matt had a long, lazy stride, but having seen him in action earlier that day, she wouldn't underestimate him. She also knew that he was not going to give up on finding out more about her as well as her parents.

She was absolutely certain that the attacks had nothing to do with them, but maybe it wouldn't hurt to let Matt and the rest of the SBS team confirm it for themselves.

In the meantime, she intended to do her best to convince them that it was her former trainer who was behind the incidents. But as sure as she was, it was troubling to think that Esquivel would resort to killing her to prevent her testifying. Especially since what he was being accused of normally only resulted in relatively minor suspensions of time.

"Penny for your thoughts, although I suspect they're worth much more than that," Matt said as he returned to the ATV and urged Butter back up into the storage box behind the two seats.

She had been so lost in those thoughts she hadn't noticed his return. "I was just thinking that Esquivel trying to shoot me is out of line with his possible punishment."

"What are they claiming he did?" Matt asked and hopped back into the driver's seat.

"I thought it was about his doping a horse. From what I've seen for similar incidents, I'm not sure they'd suspend him for more than six months or so," she explained again as they drove back to the ranch house.

"What if it's about more than that?" he asked, wheeling the ATV to a spot in the driveway in front of the house.

Teresa considered aloud what else it could be. "If it risked a horse's life or involved animal welfare claims, it could be years...but I never knew Esquivel to do anything along those lines."

Matt rocked his head back and forth, contemplating what she'd said. "Maybe we should dig a little into what he's accused of doing."

Teresa nodded. "I can look online or make some calls in the morning."

"Great. Let's get you inside. I'll make sure it's secure and then I'll take Butter for another walk around the stables."

"A walk" being a euphemism for making sure the area was safe, but she was okay with that. The constant worry about the attacks had been eating away at her. She had lost weight because her appetite was gone and hadn't really slept well in weeks.

The dinner with the SBS team was the first time in a long time that she'd been hungry and eaten anything of substance. She hoped that maybe tonight, with Matt in the house, she'd finally get some rest.

He walked her to the door, Butter at his side, and his large hand at the small of her back was surprisingly comforting.

When she unlocked the door, he urged her to stay on the porch and went in with Butter to make sure the inside was safe. Minutes later, he returned. "All good."

"I'll wait for you to get back before I turn in," she said and entered her home.

"I won't be long."

With a nod, he walked toward the stables, his easy stride taking him into the darkness. When she lost sight of him, she closed the door. Too nervous to just sit and wait, she went into her office and powered up her laptop, intending to read as much as she could about what the racing world was saying about Esquivel and his issues.

As soon as she popped in his name and did an internet search, article after article came up about her former trainer. Most of the stories speculated that the inquiries were about another of Esquivel's horses testing positive for a performance-enhancing drug. Nothing new, not that she'd known that when she'd first hired him.

Esquivel had been eager to work with her even though she didn't have an established track record. She had been grateful to have someone with his experience willing to work with a novice racehorse owner. When their first two horses had won a number of races, she'd been convinced that she'd made the right choice.

The money from the wins had helped her buy her current property as well as a foal with impressive lineage to train. She and Esquivel had trained the foal together for three years and had even more success until the horse had sliced a tendon during a race.

That was the first time that she and Esquivel had butted heads. Esquivel had wanted to have the horse euthanized for the insurance money, but she had insisted on saving the animal. It had cost her almost all her winnings from the foal to treat and rehabilitate him. Luckily, the stallion had been back on a racetrack in a little over a year and had won enough purses to make the stable profitable again.

Despite that, Esquivel had insisted that she'd made a mistake, and the continued tension between them had reached the boiling point when she walked into the stables one day and caught the trainer injecting one of her mares. Since they hadn't discussed any kind of treatment for the horse, she'd been skeptical about Esquivel's claims that it was only a vitamin injection.

She'd had Miranda take a blood sample, which had revealed the mare had been given a performance-enhancing drug. When she'd challenged Esquivel about the PED, he'd acted insulted that she would accuse him. His protestations had only worsened their relationship.

When barely a month later she'd caught him using a banned corticosteroid on another horse, she'd fired him and begun a search for a new trainer. Finding Richard was the best thing to happen to her. She loved working with him, and he had helped her build her stable into one with a solid reputation for winners.

The snick of the lock on the front door signaled that Matt and Butter were back. His footsteps and the jangle of Butter's collar grew louder as they approached her office.

"You still working?" he said, leaning an arm on the doorjamb.

She closed her laptop so she could give him her full attention. "Just trying to find out more about what's up with Esquivel."

He nodded. "Did you find out anything?"

"Surprisingly, no. I thought the articles would definitively say why the racing commission in New York would be going after him, but they didn't."

TERESA HAD AN expressive face, and it was clear from her current look that she was puzzled by the lack of information in the articles.

"You think it has to do with the doping allegations, right?" Matt asked.

With a shrug of her fine-boned shoulders, she said, "I think that's why they want to talk to me. I can't imagine what else it could be about."

"Let me know if you find anything. In the meantime, are you okay with Butter being off her leash?"

"Of course. Anything you need for the two of you to be comfortable."

"Great," he said, reached down and unclipped the leash from Butter's collar. But the dog remained at his side, tongue hanging out of her mouth, which was why the breeder had sold her off for K-9 work. No one wanted a show dog with a tongue that wouldn't stay in its mouth.

"You should try to get some rest. I'm going to man the monitors," he said with a jerk of his thumb in the direction of the nearby dining room.

"I just have a few more things to do," she said, and he could tell she was determined to find out more about her former trainer. He understood. He'd gotten the sense she didn't like relying on others and he admired that. But it also made it a little harder to just think of her as another spoiled rich girl.

"Don't work too hard," he said and stepped away to get to work and put some distance between them. Teresa was way too intriguing, and he couldn't afford to be distracted on this assignment. Too much was at stake. With that thought paramount in his mind, he headed into the dining room to keep an eye on the Redland Ranch property.

Sophie, Robbie and the SBS techs had set up the nine monitors so that he could not only view them but also look out the windows of the dining room. The far windows faced the public road and entrance onto the property. A large SBS SUV and guard sat at the gate. The windows to his right faced the driveway, pond and the stables in the distance.

Leaning his hands on the desk pad protecting the ma-hogany of the dining room table, he peered from one moni-tor to the other, getting a sense of where Sophie and Robbie had installed the various security cameras. He had eyes on the stable areas and ranch house from one set of cam-eras. Another monitor displayed the track, and several other feeds came from the trail cameras they'd positioned along the perimeter.

The monitor dead center was free to check the status of the system, search the internet or do any other computer-related task. Just to be sure, he sat down and ran a system check that confirmed all was in order with the cameras.

"It's all looking good, Butter," he said as the shepherd sat by his side. He reached over, rubbed her ears and made a fist to instruct her to lie down. She immediately responded to the hand command. "Good girl," he praised her.

Since she had been so good that day, he took out a bag of biscuits from the bag he'd brought in earlier and offered her a peanut butter and bacon treat, one of her favorites. She gobbled it up happily, bringing a smile to his lips.

Satisfied all was well on the property, he texted Sophie

to make sure he could reach her and got an almost immediate response.

"Don't you ever stop working?" he texted back.

"Do you?" she challenged, and he chuckled.

"Can you see the camera feeds?" he asked.

"I can. Let me know when you want to take a break."

In the military he'd sometimes had to go for a couple of days without any real sleep, but to stay sharp he needed at least a few hours of sleep.

"I'll catch some shut-eye in the morning if that's okay with you," he wrote back, and they agreed on a time where he could snag some rest.

He focused again on the monitors, but also felt the need to find out more about Teresa and her parents. Even though she was adamant there was no connection between what was happening and them, it just didn't make sense that the attacks were solely about Teresa testifying against her former trainer. Especially since the punishment was possibly only several months of suspension. But as Robbie had pointed out, people killed for less.

With that in mind, he did a quick search on the trainer. Several results mentioned his many suspensions over the years. That made him wonder if the racing commission hadn't decided on a much longer, even more permanent suspension in light of his history. Maybe that was what prompted the attacks and the escalation.

And yet there was still a nagging suspicion in his gut that it was about more and possibly not about the trainer.

He pulled up information on Teresa's parents and their casino, a small but exclusive property in Miami. There were a number of articles about the success of the business and a possible expansion into a second location at one of the old greyhound racetracks that had been shuttered when Florida banned dog racing.

It struck him as too coincidental that the recurring crimes on Redland Ranch and the boom in Teresa's parents' business were happening at the same time.

He kept on digging, reading up on the history of the business. The family had used to own a casino in Havana before Castro had come to power. After escaping the Communist regime like so many Cubans, the Rodriguezes had settled in Miami. After several years of struggle, they'd bought a run-down jai alai fronton and turned it around.

As popular as the ball sport had been in the sixties and seventies, it had started to see a decline in the eighties, according to the articles. There were assorted issues, including reports of murder and arson, and possible mob connections.

Teresa's family had apparently survived by doing a pivot to grow the casino side of the business while also keeping alive Miami's beloved jai alai by bringing in young athletes to play. Thanks to them and another casino, the sport was almost thriving in Miami again.

But did that mean the mob was also wanting to get in on the action again? Matt asked himself.

As much as Teresa might hate it, SBS had to investigate that possibility. He'd find a way to gently get Teresa to consider the likelihood that it was someone other than Esquivel who was trying to silence her.

While he'd been searching and reading, he'd also multitasked and kept an eye on the cameras. But so far there hadn't been any signs of activity except for Luis checking on Frijoles. Over an hour had gone by and he was getting stiff from sitting for so long. Much like Trey, he was used to being an all-action guy, so it was time for another patrol in and around the stables and the perimeter.

He shot up out of the chair and gave Butter a hand command to follow. As he walked out, he realized Teresa was still working at her laptop.

Her brow was furrowed, emerald gaze intense as she focused on the computer. The light cotton of her T-shirt clung to her delicate shoulders and stretched across generous breasts.

She really was beautiful, he thought, and battled a curl of unwanted desire as he stepped to the door of the room, needing to be close to her.

Chapter Seven

"You really should get some rest. You look worn out," Matt said as he rested a thickly muscled arm on the door jamb.

"Flatterer," Teresa teased, but hated that she hadn't been at her best in front of this man. Maybe hated even more that it mattered to her, because she wasn't interested in any kind of involvement with him.

"Just saying," he said in a laconic drawl that spoke words beyond those.

But he was right that she needed to get some rest. Shutting her laptop, she popped to her feet and said, "I just need to check on Frijoles one last time."

Matt nodded. "Butter and I will walk you over."

She found it funny he was including Butter, as if doing so made it more business than personal. But she got it—it had to stay business between them.

"Thanks. I'd like that," she said and meant it. His company—and Butter's—lessened the worry that had been dragging her down the last few weeks.

Together they strolled out of the house and over to the stables. Ay Caramba was in her stall, peacefully quiet, probably catching a nap before bedding down for a few hours.

Frijoles was up and Luis was keeping him company. As the young man saw her, he said, *"Esta mejor. Gracias a Dios."*

"Muchissimas gracias," she echoed. *"Deberías ir a descansar. Es seguro ahora que SBS está aquí."*

Luis looked from her to Matt and back to her. He nodded and said, "I'll get some rest when Frijoles goes to sleep."

She knew better than to argue with her young stable hand. Since the time she'd hired him out of a program intended to help teens break from dangerous gangs, he had been determined to prove to her that she hadn't made a mistake. Besides being a hard worker, he'd also been doing well with his GED courses, and she hoped they'd be able to get him into college once he finished.

"Hasta mañana, Luis," she said, and Matt repeated the goodbye.

As they walked back toward the ranch house, Matt asked, "Is it true horses sleep standing up?"

She looked at him in surprise, wondering how he'd been brought up. "A Texas boy who doesn't know about horses?" she teased and instantly regretted it as his features tightened, almost painfully.

"I'm sorry. I didn't mean anything by it."

He raised his hands as if to stop her. "No need. Not all of us grow up on ranches."

Not wanting to press since it seemed to upset him, she said, "Most horses lie down for a few hours of deep sleep late at night. During the day they cat nap while standing."

"Survival instinct when they used to be in the wild, I guess," he said. As his gaze met hers, she realized he'd also had to find a way to survive and found herself wanting to know more about him.

They had reached her front door and she unlocked it, but as he had before, he gestured for her to wait while he and Butter checked inside. When he returned, he dipped his head and said, "All clear. *Deberías ir a descansar."*

"I will try to get some rest. *Gracias*, Matt. *Por todo*," she said and gently brushed a hand across his jaw in thanks.

THAT FLEETING CARESS almost undid him and he tore away from her and toward the ATV to do another round of patrol.

As he had before, he commanded Butter into the passenger seat, but she tilted her head at a questioning angle, as if asking him why he was leaving Teresa.

"Come on, girl. You know she's nothing but trouble," he said and quickly pulled away from the ranch house.

He circled around the stables to the track area, moving along a different route to see if there was anything new that might provide a clue as to who was behind the incidents. Nothing. He headed to the perimeter of the property, catching sight of the first guard at his post. The man waved at him in greeting and Matt pushed on to the farthest edge of the property by the stand of trees and the second guard. Another wave said all was well and he went to the front where the third guard was in place.

Pausing there for a second, he perused the residential road that ran in front of the property and the areas all around. Across the street from the stables was a private home with a low cement wall that ran across the front of that residence. The wall could easily provide cover for someone. He carefully pulled onto the street and slowly drove across the length of the wall, keeping a close eye for anything out of the ordinary. Nothing. But something about the property niggled at him and he made a note to go over and talk to the neighbors in the morning.

He circled back to the driveway and returned to the ranch house. Walking Butter one last time for the night, he headed in and found that Teresa was still up and waiting for him in the living room. She set aside the book she'd been reading—a romance novel, he could tell from the cover—and stood.

"I didn't get a chance to show you which room to use," she said and pointed a finger upward.

He nodded and, after grabbing the duffel he'd left there earlier that day, followed her up the stairs. As they walked down the hall on the upper level, she gestured to the first bedroom they passed and said, "You can use this room. The bathroom is right next door."

Stopping by the door, he said, "And your room is…" He needed to know the lay of the land in case of an emergency, he told himself.

She pointed down the hall. "Last door on the left."

With a nod, he said, "I should get back to work. *Buenas noches.*"

"Buenas noches," she said but he had already turned and raced down the steps, eager to be back to work and away from her.

As he made himself comfortable in front of the monitors and Butter settled down close to his feet, he forced himself to focus on the images on the screens and not on thoughts of Teresa getting ready for bed. It was an epic fail as his body tightened in reaction to those visions.

A text message popped across his screen. Sophie asking, "Everything okay?"

"Everything is okay," he replied even though things were far harder than he expected. And in more ways than one, he thought with a quick glance at the unwanted bulge in his khakis.

"Calling it a night. Will come online around five so you can get some shut-eye," she texted.

"Gracias. Get some rest."

"You, too," she said even though they both knew rest would be the farthest thing on his mind with all that was going on.

THE NIGHT PASSED without incident, and at five, as promised, Sophie had texted him that she would take over. He walked Butter so she could relieve herself and went upstairs for a few short hours of sleep. Butter lay on the floor next to the bed and he set an alarm for eight, and as he'd trained himself to do in the Marines, went fast to sleep.

He woke to the chime of the alarm and took a quick shower, dressed and headed downstairs to walk Butter and feed her. As he spilled food into the bowl, he thought about last night's meal and how eagerly Teresa had eaten. He wouldn't be surprised to know that she hadn't been eating well with all that had happened. He had noticed her clothes had been loose on her and she was a little too thin despite her very nice curves.

Since she still wasn't up, he decided to make them breakfast to hopefully remedy her lack of appetite. Rummaging through her cupboards and refrigerator, he found an assortment of things he could put together for breakfast. But first coffee.

He got a pot started and heated some milk for *café con leche*. After a satisfying sip, he got to work, cooking up some onion and garlic before adding bottled salsa. Then he threw in some oregano, cumin and a bay leaf, and set the mixture to simmer. Turning on a second gas burner, he charred some corn tortillas over the flames and placed them on plates. Last night's leftover black beans, not traditional but still tasty, got mashed, heated and spread over the tortillas.

Since he'd scrounged up a ripe avocado from the fridge, he sliced it and laid the slices next to the tortillas. Finished with her breakfast, Butter padded over to sit and watch him cook. He'd sometimes give her a treat while he cooked at home, and since she'd been so good, he went to the fridge, snared a small piece of cheese and tossed it to her.

She wolfed it down and resumed her spot beside him as he gave the salsa mixture another stir. The only thing left to do was to fry the eggs. And as he heated some oil and prepped the eggs, he heard signs of life on the floor above.

He had scooped the fried eggs onto the beans and was just spreading on some of the salsa when Teresa walked into the kitchen.

She had her hair up in a ponytail and looked refreshed, her green eyes bright and free of the worry that had filled them yesterday. The T-shirt and riding pants she wore were loose on her but couldn't hide the generous curves of her breasts and hips. Black riding boots completed her outfit.

"Buenos dias," she said, her voice sleep-husky.

Desire slammed into his gut as he imagined her saying that to him in bed, but he ripped his gaze away from her and concentrated on spooning the last of the salsa on the beans as he muttered, "You must have slept well. You don't look as tired as you did yesterday."

WELL, THAT WAS *a fine "good morning,"* Teresa thought as she prepped a cup of coffee for herself. A gentleman wouldn't have pointed out that she'd looked like death warmed over, but Matt was clearly no gentleman.

It stung, making her shoot back with, "At least I don't smell today."

His hands shook as he finished working at the stove and he turned, a chagrined smile on his face.

"I'm sorry. I just meant to say you look rested. Let's try

this again. *Buenos dias*, Teresa," he said and held his hands out, as if in pleading.

Okay, maybe he wasn't a total ass. "*Buenos dias*, Matt. That smells delicious."

"Thank you. I hope you don't mind that I scrounged around to make us breakfast," he said, walked over with the plates and laid them on the kitchen table.

"I don't mind. This looks delicious. I love *huevos rancheros*." She grabbed napkins and cutlery, placed them next to the plates and took a spot at the table.

Matt sat kitty-corner to her, and she was once again struck by the size of him and his physicality. He wore an SBS T-shirt this time and it was tight across his shoulders and the hard muscles of his chest. A very nice chest, she remembered from her little crying jag of the day before.

Driving those thoughts away, she forked up some of the salsa, eggs, beans and tortilla. An explosion of flavor had her murmuring her approval. "*Dios mio*, this is so good," she said after she swallowed.

A slight trace of pink flared across his cheeks. "Thanks. *Mami* used to make me this for breakfast before I went to school and *Papi* went to work."

"She must be a good cook," she said and was unprepared for the sadness that darkened his blue eyes.

"She was. *Mami* passed when I was sixteen and then it was just me and *Papi* until I finished high school and enlisted."

"I'm sorry for your loss," she said, and he did a stilted shrug but didn't say anything. She didn't press because it was obvious that it hadn't been a good time for him and his father after his mother's death. That had likely been the reason for him joining the Marines.

The discussion cast a pall over the meal, and they finished it in silence. As he had the night before, Matt helped her clean up. His phone beeped just as they finished, and he shot a quick look at it.

"Sophie says a red Jeep is coming down the drive. Since the guard let it through, I assume—"

"That's Richard's four-by-four. He's my trainer. I'll introduce you to him," she said.

At the door she stopped to grab a riding helmet she'd left there, and Matt went to the dining room and returned with a radio. Together they walked out of the house and over to the driveway where Richard had parked his vehicle.

Richard eyed Matt warily, like a dad who had just caught an unwanted suitor sneaking out the door. Teresa understood. At times Richard had been like a second father to her. She gestured to Matt and Butter and explained, "Matt is part of the SBS team that's securing the stables. He'll be staying in one of the guest rooms until this is all over. That's his K-9 partner, Butter."

"SBS Agent Perez," Matt said and held his hand out to the older man.

Richard shook it and said, "Richard Wagner. I help Teresa train her racehorses."

After the introduction, Richard looked her way and said, "Were you still going to work Habanero today?"

She nodded. "I was. His owner is supposed to drop by later this week, and I was hoping we could show him how much he's improved."

"Is Habanero another of your racehorses?" Matt asked as they walked to the stables.

Teresa shook her head. "Just training him. He's a yearling and learning to be saddled. He's been a little skittish about having a rider on him and the owner asked me to help out."

"Teresa's a champ with the horses. She can literally make them dance," Richard said, fatherly pride in his voice.

The heat of a blush stole across her face, especially when Matt locked his gaze on her. "I'd love to see that," he said.

In the stable she first walked to check on Frijoles and Ay Caramba. To her relief, both horses were doing well. Luis was in with Frijoles, giving him his morning feeding.

Comfortable with that, she walked to Habanero's stall and put on her helmet before going in gingerly to greet the horse. "Horses are herd animals and the herd protected them in the wild," she turned to him to explain. "When threatened, it's instinctual to flee, so they're always on alert, like now. His ears and tail are up, waiting to see what happens."

She approached the horse from the left, but slightly in front so he could see her. She also kept on talking so the horse would know she was nearing him. "*Buenos dias*, Habanero. How is my boy today?" She laid a gentle hand on the side of his face.

The horse bumped her with his head, and she laughed. "Yes, you will get a treat if you're good for me today."

"I'll go get the tack," Richard said and walked away to retrieve the saddle and other equipment she would need.

But when Richard returned just a minute later, his face was hard as stone. "Someone cut up all the bridles."

Chapter Eight

Matt walked over to examine the bridle that Teresa's trainer held up.

The straps that kept the bridle on the horse's head had been slashed, making it unusable. He allowed Butter to sniff the bridle, and she began to paw the ground as a signal that she recognized a scent.

Teresa left the horse's side to also take a look and pursed her lips after examining it. "We might be able to have them repaired, but that won't help me now." She glanced back toward the horse and said, "I can't afford to lose another day of training him."

"I might have a spare one in my Jeep," Richard said and hurried off to check.

"When was the last time you used them?" Matt asked as he fingered the ruined leather straps.

"We didn't train yesterday with all that happened, so it would have been the day before."

"Whoever poisoned the feed probably did this at the same time. Explains why Butter picked up on his scent in the stable area," Matt said and patted the shepherd on the head as a reward.

Richard returned with a bright red nylon bridle and a halter and handed them to Teresa. "I'll get the rest of the gear and meet you in the paddock."

Teresa nodded and approached the horse again, walking calmly and speaking slowly so as not to spook it.

Heart pounding, Matt imagined how quickly the horse could turn and send a thousand pounds smashing into Teresa. He gripped the stall door tightly, fighting the urge to go in and protect her, but without much of a battle she had the bridle over the horse's head and the bit in place. She snapped on the halter and led the horse out of the stall, but he instructed her to wait by the door to the stables.

He grabbed a radio he had clipped to his belt on the way out the door and checked with the guards that all was clear around the perimeter. Then he texted Sophie to check as well and when she answered in the affirmative, he said, "It's safe to go out."

Teresa nodded and walked the horse to the paddock directly behind the barn.

He kept a keen eye around the property and breathed a sigh of relief when he saw nothing out of the ordinary. With a hand command, he instructed Butter to sit down.

Matt's relief was short-lived as Richard came into the paddock with a saddle blanket and saddle. At the sight of them the horse's ears shot straight up, and he started prancing nervously. Butter sensed the tension, rose to her feet and did a little growl of warning.

"It's okay, Butter. Sit," Matt commanded, and the dog looked up at him in indecision. "Sit," he repeated, his tone slightly sharper, and Butter finally listened.

Inside the paddock, Teresa crooned, "Easy, boy," and kept a steady hand on the halter, forcing the horse to calm down.

Matt's gut twisted into a knot as Richard handed her the blanket and she arranged it on the horse, controlling the large animal with only the halter and her voice. But she did subdue Habanero, exerting her dominance over him as Richard slipped on the saddle and secured it into place.

As she had earlier, she went to the horse's left side and grabbed the reins while Richard took hold of the halter. In one smooth move, Richard locked his hands together to give her a leg up and she was suddenly up in the saddle.

The horse immediately backed away from Richard nervously and did a little buck and whinny. Butter responded to the action, rising to her feet again. Matt patted her head to reassure her and ordered, "Sit." This time she immediately responded.

Teresa didn't seem fazed as the horse did another little kick of its back legs. She softly urged the horse to quiet and kept a firm hand on the reins. The muscles of her legs tightened against Habanero's sides as the horse continued to fight her, but her control didn't waver.

It was a sight to behold, the beautiful woman taming the stallion. If she had any fear, she didn't show it. Little by little the animal quieted and then slowly responded to her commands. With a soft click of her tongue, she had the horse walking around the edge of the paddock. After a few turns around, she did another little click and lightly kicked the horse's sides, and the walk became a trot.

"Good boy, Habanero. That's it," she said as they went round and round the paddock.

"She's amazing, isn't she?" Richard asked from beside him.

He had been so intent on watching Teresa in case she needed help that he hadn't realized the man had sidled up to him by the split rail fence.

"She is," he murmured, appreciative of the skill and strength it had taken to control the horse.

"Contrary to what you might think, she hasn't had it

easy," the trainer said almost offhandedly, but Matt knew it was a warning.

"She's just an assignment," he said to make things clear to the older man.

Richard scoffed and nailed him with a sharp, hazel-eyed gaze. "You know what makes a good trainer?" he said but didn't wait for Matt's reply. "Intuition and being able to read an animal. Or a person. You're interested. You're just too dense to admit it to yourself."

Before he could protest the trainer's observations, Teresa trotted up and stopped the horse before them. "We made good progress today. If we can keep up his training in the next few days, I think the owner will be pleased when he comes by."

"I think so, too," Richard said. "I can try to repair some of the bridles if you want."

Teresa shook her head. "I'm worried that would be risky. We can't have one snap during training. The outfitter should be open soon and if Matt doesn't mind, we can run over there to buy some new ones."

"Whatever you need," he said, earning a rough laugh from the trainer.

Teresa glanced between them. "Something up?"

The trainer shot him a side-eye and said, "Just talking about animals and intuition."

TERESA'S INTUITION WAS screaming that there was something going on between the two men, but she didn't get a chance to challenge them as Richard said, "If you want, I'll get him watered and cooled down so you can get the replacement bridles."

She slipped off the horse and patted his flank. His skin was damp from both their exercise and his nervousness at being ridden. "That would be great. It shouldn't take us that long to get the new equipment so I can get back to work with some of the other horses."

"See you later," Richard said with a wave of his hand. He took hold of the halter to walk the horse around the paddock.

"My car's in the garage," she said.

As they walked back toward the house, he shot her a quick glance. "Do you mind if I drive? Just in case."

She didn't need to ask what the "just in case" was. He was clearly worried about an attack.

"I don't mind. I just need to get my car keys and purse."

When they reached the house, she unlocked the front door and quickly snagged her purse, pulled out her keys and handed them to Matt.

They locked up and left the house, and she keyed in a code to open the garage door.

She was about to walk to the passenger-side door when Matt swept an arm out to hold her back. "Let us check it out first."

He walked all around the SUV with Butter sniffing the ground and car. The dog took a long time by one of the tires, prompting Matt to do a thorough inspection of the wheel well and tires, but there was apparently nothing there.

After, he lay down on the ground close to the engine and looked beneath the car, Butter inching down beside him also. Luckily it was all clear. He jumped to his feet and he and Butter examined the gas tank area before finally opening the driver's-side door and popping the hood open.

She waited patiently as he looked all around the engine and then shut the hood.

Turning to her, he said, "All clear."

She wasn't about to question his judgment as to whether

someone would try to blow her up. She had never thought someone would try to shoot her either, but they had.

Matt loaded Butter into the back and got comfortable in the driver's seat. As he pulled out of the garage and down the driveway, she gave him directions on where to turn. The shop she used for her supplies wasn't all that far away, but it was in the most rural parts of Redland and literally sat on the edge of the Everglades.

"I'll never get used to all this being so close to civilization," Matt said with a laugh as he drove.

"To be honest, me neither, but I kind of like the quiet out here," she said as he drove down a long stretch of road surrounded by a mix of wetlands and mangroves.

"I get it. The city can be a challenge at times," he admitted, but didn't elaborate for long minutes.

"Is that because you're a country boy at heart?" she asked after his prolonged silence, wanting to know more about him and not just because he was protecting her.

He did a little shrug as he competently drove the SUV into the graveled parking lot for her supplier. The SUV rocked as a tire dipped into a pothole before he parked in front of the sprawling one-story building.

"We'll go in with you," he said, obviously avoiding their earlier conversation.

She hurried into the store, Matt and Butter following close behind, his head on a swivel as they entered. Butter likewise seemed to be taking everything in but remained calm.

An older man standing at the counter waved a hand in greeting, a broad smile on his tanned and lined face. "Morning, Teresa."

"Morning, Tiny," she replied with a little wiggle of her fingers and a smile.

Tiny? Matt thought with a double take. "Tiny" was well over six feet, with shoulders almost as wide as that and a belly that bulged above a hefty silver buckle on his belt.

When he met Tiny's gaze, he realized the man was likewise giving him a once-over, obviously protective of Teresa.

Matt dipped his head to confirm he understood, and Tiny repeated the gesture.

Teresa had moved down a row in front of him and he chased after her, watching as she ran her hands over the bridles, selecting a variety of different ones.

"Aren't they all the same?" he asked.

With a little shrug of her shoulders, she held up one bridle. "This one's for Ay Caramba. She never liked having a bit in her mouth. The other ones are for training the horses for dressage, racing or just riding."

He recalled what she'd said earlier about getting back to work with the horses. "Do you race the horses? Don't you have a jockey for that?"

"We have one for the races. It would be great to have one training constantly with our horses, but usually they only come in for a day or so before a race to get used to the horse," she explained, then whirled and headed for the register.

With each thing that he learned about her, it was getting harder to think of her as a "little rich girl." Or at least as one like the woman who had ruined his life.

What kind of princess slept with her horse because it was sick or could control a powerful, thousand-pound animal through her force of will?

"Isn't that dangerous for you?" he said, imagining what might happen in a fall or if the animal bucked her off like today's horse seemed intent on doing.

She shrugged again and bobbed her head. "It can be, but

I love working with the horses, and I can't afford to have a full-time jockey on the staff."

Much like she worried she couldn't afford the services of SBS, he thought. Yet another reminder that maybe she wasn't what he had originally imagined.

At the register, Tiny raised a bushy eyebrow at the pile of bridles Teresa had placed on the counter for purchase. "Did that fire damage your tack?" Tiny asked.

He was surprised that Tiny knew about the incident. At Matt's questioning look, Teresa said, "It's a tight community."

Tiny laid a massive hand on hers as it rested on the counter. "It is and if you need me to do anything, just say the word." When he finished, Tiny looked in his direction with a warning glare.

"You don't need to worry about Teresa. She's in good hands," Matt said, provoking another glare and a lift of that hairy, very white eyebrow.

"Everything is okay, Tiny. And don't believe a word of what you hear," Teresa said, aware that news of the shooting the day before would also reach Tiny.

With a harrumph, Tiny rang up all the bridles, packed them into a large plastic bag and held it to Matt. Jabbing a finger in Matt's face, he said, "You take good care of her."

"You don't need to worry about her," Matt repeated and snagged the bag from Tiny's beefy hand.

Matt placed a protective hand at the small of Teresa's back and applied gentle pressure to guide her out of the store. With a click of the key fob, he opened the doors of her SUV, loaded Butter and the bag into the back seat, and got behind the wheel. Once Teresa was in and buckled up, he swiveled to face her.

"You have a lot of friends." The dedicated Gonzalez family, the overprotective Tiny, her loyal trainer Richard, stable hand Luis who adored her and who knew how many others.

A slight flush of color worked over her cheeks, and it had nothing to do with the sun-heated interior of the car.

"We should get going. I have a lot of work to do," she said and motioned with her index finger to the start button.

"Got it." He understood. He really wasn't into sharing about his past or his present, for that matter.

He started the car and cool air immediately blew out of the vents, chilling the heat and the awkward tension that had built between them.

Wheeling away from the store, he traveled back in the direction of the stables, but he had gone no more than a few miles when he caught sight of a white Jeep in the rearview mirror. It was moving very fast, making him keep a keen eye on it. As it neared, he caught sight of the laughing man and woman inside. Then the Jeep whipped around them and sped down the empty road in front of them.

He relaxed his grasp on the wheel, tension leaving him as the fear of danger passed.

But then he caught sight of an airboat skimming along the surface of the waterway beside the road.

It wasn't unusual to see one in the Everglades, but something about this one...

A heartbeat later the airboat surged onto the road behind them, the metal of the hull shrieking as it traveled across the pavement and clipped the back bumper. Butter reacted in the back seat, shooting to her feet and barking at the airboat.

The steering wheel jerked in his hands as he fought to keep the SUV on the road while the airboat shoved ever harder against the bumper, trying to drive them into the deadly waters beside them.

Chapter Nine

Teresa gripped her seat as the SUV fishtailed from side to side on the road, the groan of metal buckling as the airboat continued to push against their rear end.

Her heart jumped in her chest and fear tightened her throat until she could barely squeak out, "Matt?"

"Hold on. Just hold on," Matt said, hands white-knuckled on the steering wheel as he fought for control.

Risking a quick glance behind her, she caught sight of Butter jumping from side to side on the back seat and barking as the masked man operating the airboat rammed against their bumper, working the controls to try to drive them into the water.

The SUV's engine roared as Matt stomped on the accelerator, sending the car rocketing forward and away from the airboat. With that tiny bit of breathing space between them, Matt whipped the SUV to the right and away from the water's edge. The vehicle tipped up precariously on two wheels before landing with a thud and crashing into the thick underbrush.

"Stay inside," he shouted. Then he threw open his door, whipped out his gun and fired at the airboat rider as he whirled to attack them again.

The driver's body jerked as a bullet apparently struck home.

Matt shot at him again, but the driver circled the airboat around, using the whirring blades to send a blinding cascade of air and debris in their direction.

Matt flinched as the barrage hit him, but Butter and Teresa were protected in the interior of the car. It let her catch a fleeting glimpse of the airboat as it bumped across the road, metal grating and sparking against the pavement until the airboat shot down the embankment and into the waters and grass of the Everglades. But her glance was enough to see that Matt *had* wounded the man. There had been a trail of blood down his left arm.

With the threat gone, Matt holstered his weapon and leaned into the car. "You okay?"

She tried to speak but couldn't. Her throat was still tight with fear, and she could barely hear past the pounding of her heartbeat reverberating in her ears. Nodding, she sucked in a shaky inhale before finally blowing out a rough breath.

"Okay. I'm okay."

With a slight incline of his head, he said, "I need to call this in to SBS and the police, so sit tight."

Sit tight? She didn't think she'd be able to take a step she was still so shaken. But she knew she had to do something to help out. She sat there, replaying everything that had happened. Trying to remember every little detail so she could provide that to the SBS agents and the police when they arrived.

The blaring sound of sirens approaching dragged her from the increasingly stuffy and hot interior of the SUV. She'd been so intent on remembering what had happened that she hadn't realized Matt had been all up and down the road with Butter, trying to find whatever evidence they could.

As the police pulled up just in front of the SUV, he walked over to the cruiser, and she hurried over to join them.

It was Officer Ventura and her partner again. While Ventura took their statements, her partner walked the roadway, arms akimbo, his head tucked down as he perused the asphalt and embankment.

"The airboat approached you from which direction?" Ventura asked.

Matt glanced at the Everglades and pointed at the waters. "From the southwest. From deeper in the Everglades."

That was met with a shrug from Ventura as if it was the only way it could have come. "Did you catch any part of the registration numbers?" the young officer asked.

Matt nodded. "FL and I think eight-two-two something." He shook his head and drove a hand through the wavy strands of his hair in frustration. "I was too busy trying to keep the car on the road."

"Three-two-two-five followed by an H and H, I think," Teresa said, remembering what she had seen as the airboat raced away from them.

"What about the driver? What can you tell me about him?" Ventura pressed.

"White male wearing a plain white T-shirt. Dark pants. Based on how he was sitting, I'd say he was over six feet. Muscular build. I think I shot him," Matt advised.

"You did. He was hurt. I could see blood on his left arm as he drove away," Teresa said and gestured to where she had seen the wound.

"We'll put in a call to local hospitals and doctors to see if anyone comes in for treatment. As for the airboat, if he didn't take any steps to conceal the numbers—"

"He probably stole it," Matt finished for the policewoman.

"Probably. Anything else you can think of, call me," Officer Ventura said and walked away to join her partner, not that Teresa thought they'd get anything useful from the scene.

Matt faced her and cupped her cheek. "You did good remembering the registration numbers."

His touch filled her with immediate comfort, and she reached up, tenderly stroked his face with her hand. "I had to do something while you were saving our butts," she said with a ghost of a smile and a sharp laugh.

A black Suburban pulled up behind the police cruiser and a second later Trey and Mia exited the vehicle. Trey stopped to chat with the two police officers while Mia hurried over to them.

"You're all okay?" Mia asked. Her glance darted from one to the other and down to where Butter patiently sat beside Matt.

Teresa nodded. "We're okay thanks to Matt."

Mia smiled and laid a hand on Matt's shoulder. "Maybe you should head back to the stables. I'm sure you have things to do, Teresa. Trey and I will finish up here."

With a quick dip of her head, she said, "I'd like that."

MIA HELD UP the keys to the Suburban. "Take our vehicle. CSI will be here soon to get whatever evidence they can from Teresa's SUV."

Matt nodded and slipped the keys from Mia's fingers. "Please keep us posted."

"We will," Mia said and together they all walked back in the direction of the police cruiser. As Mia peeled off to join Trey and the police officers, Teresa headed to the Suburban while Butter and Matt detoured to get the bag with the bridles.

Once they were settled in the larger vehicle, Matt drove the short distance to the stables and parked in the circular driveway in front of the ranch house. As he killed the engine, he looked at Teresa. "Are you really okay?"

Teresa sucked in a long breath, but then expelled it and nodded. "I am. Scared. Again."

He was about to say something when Teresa's phone rang. Her brow furrowed as she looked at the number but then didn't answer.

"Spam call?" he asked.

"Probably," she said, and they stepped out of the car. But as they walked toward the stables, her phone dinged to announce a voice mail.

Teresa paused and glanced at the phone, clearly puzzled. "They left a message."

Matt glanced down and noticed that the voice mail had lasted over a minute. Far longer than just a phone spammer might hang on. "Put it on speaker and play it," he said and tacked on, "Please."

She did as he asked, and a man's voice erupted from the phone. "Teresa, please. Please pick up. I need to talk to you. This is serious. You can't imagine how serious. Please call me back."

"Esquivel?" Matt asked as the voice mail ended.

"Esquivel," she confirmed, hands shaking.

He gripped her hands and stroked his thumbs across her skin, trying to calm her. "You can handle him."

She worried her lower lip with her teeth and did a few quick nods. "I can. Should I call him back?"

"Not yet. Let's wait for Trey and Mia to get here. You said you had some work to do." Keeping busy would help her not to think about Esquivel's call.

Offering him a weak smile, she said, "Work would be good. We normally train the horses in the morning, but with everything that's happening, our schedules are all off."

"Lead the way," he said and followed her to the stables. Richard was inside Ay Caramba's stall with Luis and attractive older woman he assumed was the vet. The vet was running her hands across the mare's swollen belly while gently talking to the horse.

"That's a good girl. You're going to be a mama real soon," the woman said, a soothing tone in her voice.

Teresa walked to the entrance of the stall and gestured toward the woman. "Matt, this is Dr. Miranda Ramirez. Our vet," Teresa said, and Matt dipped his head in greeting.

"How is Ay Caramba doing?"

Miranda smiled and kept on stroking the horse. "Any day now, Teresa. The foal is in the right place, and everything looks good."

"That's great to hear. Did you get a chance to check out Frijoles?" Teresa asked.

Miranda nodded. "I did and he's doing well. I'd give him another day of rest before taking him out for some light exercise. I've got to run, but I'll drop by again in the next few days to see how things are going."

"Thank you. You've made my day," Teresa replied and the relief in her voice was palpable as the vet walked away.

"I want to exercise Helado. Would you help me get him ready, Richard?" Teresa said, and at Richard's nod, she turned and walked toward another stall.

Matt walked beside her and said, "Helado? As in ice cream?"

Teresa grinned. "As in ice cream. He's almost all white and the first thought I had when I saw him was that he looked like vanilla ice cream."

Matt laughed. "I guess you were having a craving when he was born."

Teresa joined in his laughter. "I was. It had been a long

night while we waited for him, and it was hot, and I was hungry for something cool."

She stopped by Frijoles's stall and the stallion came up to the door to greet her. She stroked his face. "Good to see you're feeling better, boy."

The horse blew out a breath, almost as if in response. "I know you don't like just lying around. I'll take you out tomorrow morning," she promised him as she stroked his head again.

Then they walked down a few stalls to where a beautiful white horse poked his head out of the stall.

"Helado," Teresa greeted the horse, who tossed his head, sending the paler strands of his white mane into motion. She opened the stall door and stepped inside just as Richard came over with the tack for the horse. In no time Richard and Teresa had saddled the horse and Teresa walked him out of the stall.

"He is a handsome boy," Matt said and stood beside Teresa. Butter sat at his feet but seemed restless.

Teresa glanced down at the shepherd and Matt stroked the dog's head. "You okay, Butter?"

The dog did a sharp, short woof, worrying Matt. He rose and looked all around, searching for what might be upsetting the shepherd. Nothing seemed out of the ordinary in the stables. Just to be on the safe side, he said, "Let me clear the way to make sure everything's fine."

He walked ahead of them, Butter straining on the leash in front of him, decidedly anxious about something. As they paused at the door of the stables, a sudden motion on the ground to the right had him whipping his weapon out of his holster.

Just a cat, a black-and-white blur racing away from the stables.

Butter tugged at the leash, wanting to give chase, but Matt held her back. Then the shepherd quieted and sat at his feet patiently, tongue lolling out of her mouth while she waited for Matt's command.

He shook his head. "Was that it? Just a cat?" he asked the dog, who looked up at him, totally peaceful. Almost smiling.

"You and I are going to have to work on that," he said, thinking that his K-9 partner and he still had a lot to learn about each other.

With a wave at Teresa and Richard, he said, "Just a cat. I'm sorry."

Teresa smiled and walked up to him, holding Helado's halter. "Black-and-white?" she asked.

Matt nodded as they started walking toward the track.

"That's Big Ben. He's one of our mousers," she explained and drew open a gate to enter the track area.

MATT AND BUTTER stood by the open gate as Richard hurried past them and helped her up into the saddle.

With a slight kick to Helado's side, she walked him onto the track, and with another kick, she urged him into a trot around the track until she neared the spot where Richard stood with Matt and Butter.

The trainer raised his hand and gave her a signal to push the horse into a gallop. She shifted her weight forward, rose up in the saddle, and with the urging of her hands on the reins, she pushed him faster. Mentally she counted down a two-minute lick as the horse did the first mile around the track. With the eight furlongs completed, she was almost back to where Richard, Matt and Butter waited.

Richard flashed her another signal and she pushed the

horse toward the rail and into his fastest speed, hugging the rail as they breezed around the track.

Sweat dripped down her face but she was instantly cooled by the air rushing past her as they raced through the afternoon. Life was a blur of greens and browns, and in that blur, she could forget for a moment all that was happening.

The shift of the horse's muscles beneath her was powerful, but she remained in control, riding higher in the stirrups and close to Helado's neck. His mane flew in the air, the soft strands whipping her face.

She pushed Helado, pushed herself, until she knew it was time to slow and cool him down.

Little by little she slackened his pace until they were at an easy walk around the track. Normally she'd hop off and let Luis or another of the stable hands walk the animals, but today she stayed on, relishing the time with the animal and the freedom from her current problems.

But as the sky darkened, warning that one of those typical tropical afternoon showers was on the way, she turned in and walked toward the trio waiting for her.

As she slipped off the horse, Richard said, "That was a good workout. Helado's times are improving quickly."

She smiled, pleased by that. "Sounds like we'll be able to race him this season."

Richard stroked the horse's shoulder and then moved lower past Helado's breast to his legs until he reached his fetlock. "All good. No sign of that earlier inflammation."

"That's good news," she said just as a rumble of thunder warned they should get inside.

They hurried into the stables and Richard said, "I'll take care of him. You should go get some rest."

"Thanks. I will," she said and as they headed back toward the house, Matt placed a hand at the sweat-damp small of her back. The touch was both possessive and protective and she didn't mind it.

"You were amazing out there," he said, obvious surprise and pride in his voice.

She tried to picture how he must have seen her but couldn't. To her today had been just another training session. With a hesitant shrug, she said, "*Gracias*, but it was just a regular day."

JUST A REGULAR day on an animal moving at least thirty miles an hour, if he had to guess. With nothing but a helmet on her head, which made him say, "I noticed you didn't have a whip."

"You mean a crop?" she asked, and at his nod, she explained, "I don't use one and I prefer that my jockeys don't either. It's a tough call because sometimes you need to possibly use it to prevent a collision, but I feel you can control the horse without it."

They had reached the end of the driveway and Butter pulled on the leash and began to paw the ground, clearly picking up a scent.

He stopped and laid a gentle hand on Teresa's arm to stop her. "Let Butter track this scent before the rain comes and we possibly lose it." Squatting, he rubbed the dog's ears and said, "Good girl. Find it, Butter."

He expected the shepherd to head toward the burned tack shed as it had the day before, but after sniffing around the area, Butter surprised him and headed up the driveway toward the entrance to the ranch. Head down, clearly on the scent, Butter moved to the road with Matt and Teresa following.

Pausing to make sure the road was clear of traffic, he let Butter cross over to the low wall marking the entrance to the neighbor's property and stopped there to make sure the area was clear. Before they moved forward, he said, "Do you think the neighbors will mind?"

Teresa shook her head. "They wouldn't but they're away. They're visiting their daughter and won't be home for another couple of weeks."

Matt bent and examined the tire tracks leading to the home. They looked similar to the tracks for the shooter's car that had been parked in the nearby avocado grove, but there was no car anywhere in sight.

Had the shooter made his escape across the neighbor's property or possibly even used it to hide?

Matt wasn't taking any chances. He pulled his weapon from the holster and glanced at Teresa. "Please stay here."

She shook her head vehemently, making the straps on her helmet swing with the movement. "No way. I'm going with you."

He was about to argue, but when his gaze locked with hers, the determination in her emerald eyes told him she would not relent.

Muttering a curse beneath his breath, he said, "Stay behind me."

Giving Butter another find command, he followed the shepherd as it ran the length of the wall in one direction and then doubled back to the driveway. There the dog went straight toward the house with Matt chasing after her and Teresa tucked safely behind him in case their attacker was in the house.

But as they approached safely, the heavens that had been threatening rain erupted, sending a deluge to soak them. The force of the storm was so powerful that it lashed them with rain as they stood by the door on the front porch, trying to shelter.

Shivering from the cold of the rain and teeth chattering, Teresa said, "There's a key under that flowerpot."

Matt lifted the pot with the wilted pink flowers but there was no key beneath it. Glancing at Teresa, he put his index finger to his mouth to urge her to silence and then pointed to the large window next to the door. If someone was inside, they would have seen them rush to the porch to avoid the storm, and he wanted her out of the line of fire.

Beside him, Butter was pawing at the door, alerting him that she had picked up the scent. He urged Butter back from the door so she would be out of harm's way as well and carefully turned the knob. With the nudge of his sneakered foot, he kicked the door open.

The door rebounded against the far wall with a soft thud.

Matt held his breath, waiting for an attack. Dead silence followed.

He carefully moved into the doorway, Butter tucked close to his side in case he needed to give the attack command. They breached the doorway where they'd be most vulnerable, but as he entered, it was clear that no one was in the home.

Stepping outside to where Teresa waited, arms wrapped around herself against the chill of the rain, he said, "It's all clear."

She hurried in as he examined the open-concept space that held a comfortable living room, kitchen and dining area. A plate with a few cigarette butts rested on the surface of the table beside a dirty, old-fashioned glass and bottle of rum. Beside him, Butter was pawing the ground, confirming that she had gotten the scent of their suspect.

"The Hendersons don't smoke," Teresa said.

Matt peered at the plate. The butts were from the same brand as they'd found in the shed. He observed the glass carefully. The fingerprints on its surface were obvious. "He left some nice evidence for us. If the police didn't get anything the first time, they will now."

"G-g-g-o-o-d-d," she said, teeth knocking together loudly, drawing his attention.

She was shivering, her body vibrating with cold as water dripped off her onto the terra cotta tile floor.

He muttered another curse and said, "We have to get you warm."

Leading her into the living room area, he grabbed a throw from the back of the couch and wrapped her in it. Since the storm continued to lash the house with wind and rain, he urged her onto the couch and flipped the switch by the fireplace to ignite the gas jets. Nothing happened.

"P-p-pilot-t-t is p-p-prob-b-bab-bly off," she said as she took off her riding helmet and laid it on the coffee table.

His phone started chirping and he yanked it from his wet jeans pocket. It was Mia calling. When he answered, she said, "We're at the house. Where are you?"

"Across the way at the neighbors'. Butter picked up the attacker's scent and it seems as if he's been here. Left cigarette butts and a dirty glass for us to analyze. Also, some tire tracks in front." He walked to shut the door against the rain that continued to pound the house.

"We'll call the police. Storm may take another half hour to clear, though. Are you dry and safe for now?" she asked.

He glanced at Teresa, who was still shaking from the wet and chill. "We're safe. Dry not so much. We'll stay here until the police arrive."

"We'll have some warm food waiting for you when you get here," Mia said and ended the call.

He issued a hand command for Butter to stay, and before she settled herself down, she shook the rain off her short fur.

Returning to Teresa, he sat beside her and scooped her up into his lap.

She came without protest and burrowed into his warmth.

He wrapped his arms around her and little by little her body stopped shaking. She peered up at him, and this close he could see the lighter green shards in the depths of those jewel-tone eyes. And that perfect nose and those full lips. Natural lips, not fake, model ones.

She can be a model, she is so beautiful, he thought, cupped her cheek and ran his thumb across those tempting lips.

TERESA HAD BEEN grateful for the heat his body had provided, but now there was a different kind of heat building between them.

The butterfly-light pass of his thumb on her lips was as intimate as any kiss, and her body responded to it, nipples tightening against her damp T-shirt. Heat and wet pooled at her center.

It had been too long since she'd been with a man, and it hadn't been a man like Matt. Big. Hard-bodied. Complex. She mimicked his action and cupped his jaw.

His skin was beard-rough beneath her palm. Hard much like the rest of him, but as she met his gaze, it was impossible to miss the need in his sapphire eyes.

Need that mirrored her own and she wasn't about to deny him or herself.

Bending, she covered his lips with hers, moaning at the feel of them and his muscled body against hers.

He returned the kiss, meeting her lips over and over until it wasn't enough, and he opened his mouth on hers with a soft groan.

His growing hardness registered against the softness of her hip and her insides pulsed with need as she imagined being with him.

The loud pounding of a fist on the front door and Butter issuing sharp, insistent barks had them jerking apart and shooting to their feet.

Her rough breathing sounded harsh and overly loud to her ears as Matt raced over and jerked the door open.

Chapter Ten

She inhaled sharply and ran shaky hands down her wet riding pants, trying to tamp down the desire racing through her body. Wrapping the throw around herself to hide any telltale signs of her need.

Idiot. You shouldn't have done that, she told herself as Matt let Officer Ventura and her partner into the house. With a short wave of his hand, he instructed Butter to come with them.

Matt led the officers over to the table and they stood there, water dripping off their hats and raincoats. Officer Ventura looked her way and said, "You say your neighbors aren't home?"

Teresa nodded. "They left over a week ago to visit their daughter."

Ventura said, "We'll bag this evidence and have the CSI lab analyze it. I have no doubt that they'll be able to get something from it. Once the rain lets up, we'll call them to take a look at the tire tracks as well, but they look like a pretty common pattern. At best they'll be able to confirm if they're the same as the shooter's in the avocado grove."

Her partner nodded and said, "Too bad they don't have a doorbell camera. We might have gotten a picture of the suspect."

"How do you think the suspect drove past you without you seeing him coming and going? This house is right across the way." Ventura gestured in the direction of the front door and the clear view all the way to Teresa's home.

Matt shrugged and dragged a hand through the waves of his hair in obvious frustration.

But it suddenly occurred to Teresa how that had happened. "This property was a farm that has another road in the back. It leads to a small barn on the outskirts of the old farm."

The male officer, whose name she didn't recall ever getting, faced her and said, "We'll have CSI check that area out as well."

She read the name tag on his dark blue shirt. "*Gracias*, Officer Smith."

He tipped his head and shot a look toward the door. "Rain's let up. If you don't have anything to add about what's happened here, you're free to go."

"Thanks, we'll let you get to work. We appreciate everything you're doing," she said with a smile.

Matt's gut twisted with jealousy as Teresa smiled at the officer, especially as the young man launched a too friendly grin back at her.

"Yes, let's go," Matt said and laid a possessive hand on her back. Applying gentle pressure, he guided her to the door, and they walked in silence to her house, Butter tucked close to his side. When he opened the door, the sounds of Trey and Mia filtered out along with the smell of something garlicky and earthy.

Inside, Mia was at the stove cooking while Trey stood at the counter, chopping lettuce. He looked up as they entered. "We were just making dinner. Roni, Sophie and Robbie should be here soon."

Mia half turned from the stove, wooden spoon dripping with tomato sauce poised over the pan. "You should get changed and comfortable. Dinner won't take long. Just some spaghetti and meatballs."

With a quick awkward glance in his direction, Teresa said, "It smells great. *Gracias*."

"Yes, thanks. We'll be back shortly," Matt said as Teresa wasted no time heading up the stairs, but at the door to her room, she paused, hesitant. Uncertain.

"About what just happened," she began in a low whisper and with a nervous glance down the stairs.

He held his hands up and waved them in a stop gesture. "It's okay, Teresa. It was just…we got carried away. It didn't mean anything," he said even though it had.

A flicker of pain drifted across her eyes before she shuttered her emotions. In a tight voice, she whispered, "Sure. Nothing. It meant nothing."

Before he could take it back, she whirled and almost slammed the door in his face.

Butter did a little bark, drawing his attention. The dog looked up at him and even there he detected annoyance with his behavior.

"Are you ladies all sticking together?" he said, and with a low whistle, asked Butter to go with him to the bathroom where he snagged a towel and rubbed the dog dry. Returning to the guest room, he took her off the leash and instructed her to lie down so she could get some rest after all that had happened that day.

Grabbing fresh clothes, he hurried to the bathroom, showered and changed.

Butter raised her head as he walked to the door of the guest room, instantly alert. "Come here, girl," he said, and when she did, he bent to rub her ears the way she liked. The dog smiled and he fixed his gaze with hers and whispered, "I promise not to be such an idiot."

Butter woofed out a short bark and wagged her head back and forth as if accepting that promise.

Together they went down the stairs and to the kitchen, where Matt gave Butter a fresh bowl of water and a serving of food. She immediately buried her head in the bowl, gobbling up the kibble.

"Is there anything I can do?" he asked since everyone was at work in the kitchen. Teresa was helping Mia with the pasta while Trey was still at the counter of the peninsula.

Trey half turned in his direction. "Why don't you set the table?"

"Sure," he said to his boss, only it was hard to think of Trey that way in a setting like this. Trey had turned his attention to chopping up some cucumbers and tomatoes for the salad, and again it struck Matt how odd it was that the family combined their work with everyday routines like this. But maybe that was how they managed to survive when work could consume so much of one's life.

It had certainly taken over Trey's life when he'd been a cop much as it had Matt's. Long days and sometimes even longer nights had eaten into his personal life, which was maybe why he hadn't had a relationship in what seemed like forever.

That's why I responded to Teresa the way I did, he told himself. Only the little voice in his head screamed, "Liar!"

As Teresa brushed past him to place a bowl on the table, her fresh scent teased his senses, sending his body into overdrive. He sucked in a breath to tamp his need down, but only managed to draw in even more of that potent aroma.

She stopped in front of him, her gaze puzzled. "Everything okay?"

He didn't trust himself to speak; his voice was so tight with the emotion he was fighting. Nodding, he turned away from her to fiddle with the cutlery he had already set, and she walked to Trey's side.

WELL, IF HE wants to avoid me, I can do the same, Teresa thought. She grabbed the salad bowl from Trey and took it to the table.

Matt stood there, hands clasped in front of him while he rocked back and forth on his heels, clearly uncomfortable.

She fought back making a comment. She didn't want Mia and Trey to think something was up, because it could affect Matt's employment and because she knew Mia would pick up on it.

Luckily the ringing of the video doorbell Sophie and Robbie had installed gave her an excuse and she headed to the front door. To her surprise, Butter, who had been lazing by her food bowl, hopped to her feet and hugged her side protectively as she went to the door.

While she walked, she checked who was at the door on her smartphone. It was the Gonzalez tech gurus, and she opened the door with a smile. "Works like a charm," she said and waved her phone in the air.

"Glad to hear," Sophie said and hugged her before she stepped inside.

Robbie likewise embraced her and said, "Heard you had an eventful day."

"You could say that," Teresa replied, as always surprised by Robbie's unrestrained candor, which could at times be off-putting.

He wrapped an arm around her shoulder and hugged her again. "It'll get better. Trust us."

His easy tone and the comforting weight of his hug alleviated some of her earlier upset at his offhand comment.

"I do trust you," she said and truly meant it. As crazy as things had become in a matter of days, it would have been far worse without the presence of SBS and Matt. But even though Matt had saved her from physical danger repeatedly, he also presented a different kind of danger. One that could be as risky as the first.

They had barely reached the kitchen when the doorbell rang again, but Matt was already yanking out his smartphone to check. "It's Roni and John. I'll let them in." He rushed away, almost as if he was afraid to spend too much time in her presence.

She tried not to let it hurt and busied herself with adding another setting for John Wilson, Mia's newlywed husband, and helping Mia finish cooking the pasta so they could dole out heaping bowls of pasta and sauce to go with the meatballs and salad they had already placed on the table.

Welcoming Roni and John as they walked in, she was joined by Mia, who kissed her husband and said, "I wasn't expecting you tonight."

"I know how your family can be on an important case and figured this was the only way I'd get to see you for dinner," he said, wrapped an arm around her to draw her close and dropped a kiss on her forehead.

Teresa had met John a few times at other Gonzalez family events, but there was a relaxed air around him now that she hadn't sensed during their earlier meetings. His hazel eyes gleamed with joy when they settled on his wife just as Mia's azure eyes glittered happily with his presence.

As Trey joined Roni, he laid a possessive hand on the small bump of her belly and kissed her tenderly.

Teresa's heart constricted with a tumble of emotions at the sight of the two happy couples. Happiness. Sadness. Hope.

Dragging her gaze from them, she returned to the pot with the pasta just as the kitchen timer dinged to warn it was time to drain off the water. She shut off the gas and was about to grab pot holders to lift the heavy pot, but Matt was suddenly there to help.

"It's heavy," he said and moved the pot to the sink to empty the contents into a colander. When he finished, he transferred the pasta back to the pot and returned it to the stove.

Together they prepped bowls of pasta and served them as the family members set out sodas and water and then settled around the table, leaving two spots side by side for her and Matt.

Reluctant to be near him despite their teamwork on the meal, she had no choice but to sit and make the best of the situation. As it had the day before, her hunger awoke with the tasty smells of the food and the company of the Gonzalez family.

Their initial talk around the table revolved around John's new software program and Roni's visit to the obstetrician, but as the pasta bowls slowly emptied, the discussion turned to everything else that had happened that day.

"The police have confirmed that the airboat was stolen from a tourist company just a few miles away," Roni said as she twirled up a final forkful of the spaghetti.

"If he was watching us from the neighbor's property, he knew we were going somewhere, but not where," Teresa offered for consideration.

"Except he might have seen Richard go to his car for that bridle and assumed we'd be going to get new ones," Matt said.

"Or he may have a tracking device on your car," John said and glanced at Sophie and Robbie. "Do you have an RF detector with you?"

"I probably have one in the trunk," Robbie said. His fork clinked against his empty bowl. "Is there more?"

"In the pot," Teresa said, and Robbie hopped up to refill his dish.

"He's a bottomless pit," Sophie said with a shake of her head, prompting chuckles from the family members.

"I guess I am as well, especially since I'm eating for two," Roni said and rose to get more pasta, but Trey laid a gentle hand on her shoulder and said, "I'll get it for you."

That mix of emotions tugged at Teresa again at the warmth and easygoing nature of the family and the way they could mix their business with family as Sophie said, "We'll check Teresa's car after dinner."

MATT WAS GRATEFUL Sophie had shifted the discussion back to work. He didn't really know how to handle the family part since he hadn't had much of a family life once his mother had died. After that family dinners had usually been silent events, with his father sitting there slowly getting drunk while he shoveled in whatever simple meal Matt had managed to rummage together from the meager groceries in the house.

"What about the partial fingerprint? Any luck with that?" Matt asked, determined to move the investigation along so that Teresa could go back to her normal life and so could he. She was just too much of a temptation and he didn't know how much longer he could resist.

Roni said, "It was only a partial and smudged, but they think they have a suspect." She paused and gazed at Teresa in a way that had him worrying about what she would say next, and he wasn't wrong to worry.

"The suspect is Finn Walker, a low-level criminal with mob connections. This is his mug shot." Roni swiped open her smartphone and handed it to Teresa, who narrowed her gaze to peer at the photo.

Teresa shook her head and passed the phone back to Roni. "He doesn't look familiar."

"Walker has served time for bookmaking, money laundering, assault and loan sharking. He works for Tony Hollywood," Roni said, which earned a low whistle from Trey.

"Tony Hollywood is trouble. He's a big deal in the mob world and that makes me wonder what he wants with Teresa," Trey said.

Teresa's tension at the mention of the mob registered as her body stiffened beside him. As much as he didn't want to take the discussion there, he had to, because it was the only thing that made sense.

"What if what he wants has more to do with Teresa's parents," he said.

Teresa reacted in anger as she had the night before. "My parents have nothing to do with the mob," she said with a sharp slash of her hand.

Matt took hold of that hand and applied gentle pressure to reassure her as he said, "And maybe that's the problem. Maybe the mob is using you to get to your parents."

"That's a possible scenario, but if they were threatening harm to Teresa, wouldn't her parents have warned her?" Mia glanced at those sitting around the table, clearly inviting their thoughts.

"Have you told your parents about what's happening?" Sophie asked.

Teresa shook her head. "I didn't want to worry them."

Mia jumped in with, "Which means if they did get a threat and thought that nothing was happening—"

"They wouldn't believe there was really a threat," Trey finished for her.

"And they probably wouldn't say anything to Teresa so she wouldn't worry," Matt said and squeezed Teresa's hand again to offer support, since she was clearly troubled by where the investigation was going.

He was therefore surprised when she said, "I think it's time we talked to my parents."

Chapter Eleven

Teresa sat silently in the passenger seat as Matt pulled up to her parents' casino in the West Miami area.

"Are you ready?" he asked, obviously aware of how difficult a conversation this would be.

The pressure in her chest nearly cut off her breath, but she managed to say, "I am."

They exited her SUV, which had been checked for a tracking device the night before by Sophie, Robbie and John. They had found a small device buried in a hard-to-see area in the wheel well that Butter had hesitated over. To make sure the car wouldn't be tracked again, the trio had fashioned a wireless detector that would warn them if the car was compromised.

Beside her, Matt's head was a on a swivel, constantly on alert to look for any danger, Butter at his side. She wondered if he'd ever been to the casino and if not, what he'd make of it and her parents.

"Have you ever been here before?" she asked as they walked up the steps to the front doors. Palm trees and lush foliage lined the edges of the sidewalks and steps, giving the area a very tropical vibe.

"No, I haven't. I'm not much of a gambler."

"I'm not either. My parents built this to look just like the family casino in Cuba," she said. The front facade of the neoclassic structure had several doorways on both floors with semicircular windows above each door and a balcony that ran the length of the second floor. In the center of the building was an ornate triangular pediment featuring her family's coat of arms.

"It has that vibe. I've seen pictures of buildings like this in Cuba," he said, holding the door open for her.

"Gracias," she said. They entered the casino and were immediately assaulted by the cacophony of noise from the slot machines and gaming tables. A security guard approached them as he took note of Butter, but then backed away when he realized the dog was with Teresa.

They pushed to the back of the building, which held a large jai alai fronton.

She paused at the glass wall that separated the fronton from the rest of the casino. A wide swath of stadium-style seating held many spectators watching the players in the glass-enclosed court whip the ball around using handheld wicker *cestas*.

"They're very fast," Matt said as he also viewed the action on the fronton.

Teresa nodded. "Some say it's the fastest ball sport in the world."

MATT COULD BELIEVE it as the men with the long baskets on their hands caught the ball in those baskets and sent it speeding across the walls of the court. They watched for a few minutes more until Teresa said, "My parents' office is right off the fronton area."

She gestured with a hand to the side of the building where a guard stood by a door, hands clasped before him while his keen eyes kept vigilant for anything out of the ordinary. The stern look on his face faded as he caught sight of Teresa.

"*Señorita* Teresa. So good to see you again," he said with a broad smile and held the door open for them. Past the doors there was a reception area where a young Latina manned the desk. She also smiled as she saw Teresa and said, "Your parents are waiting for you."

"*Gracias*, Yolanda," she said, but paused at the door to her parents' office. Glancing at him over her shoulder, she said, "Are you ready?"

Ready as I'll ever be, he thought and nodded.

They walked into a very modern, luxurious and unusual office. Two large desks sat at either side of the room, facing each other. Behind each desk were bookcases filled with an assortment of books, photos and other mementos.

Along the wall, perpendicular to the two desks, was a seating area with a leather couch, two chairs and a coffee table. An older couple sat on the couch and rose as they entered.

The woman sauntered over, hugged Teresa and kissed each cheek. "*Mi'ja, tan bueno verte,*" she said.

"It's good to see you, too, *Mami*," Teresa said as her mother came to stand before him. She was slightly shorter than Teresa, even with the three-inch heels she wore, and her dark brown hair was in a short bob that framed a perfectly made-up face, which had barely a wrinkle. She perused him and Butter at length before extending a bejeweled hand with gold bracelets that dangled at her wrist. "Raquel Rodriguez. I'm Teresa's *madre*."

He hadn't needed her to tell him, since the two women bore a strong resemblance. They had the same nose and chin, but Teresa's mother had dark brown eyes and not Teresa's amazing emerald color. "*Señora* Rodriguez. *Encan-*

tado de conocerte," he said even though he suspected her parents weren't happy to meet him.

While he'd been greeting her mother, Teresa's father had come over to heartily hug his daughter and now shifted to greet him.

He was an imposing man, almost as tall as Matt, with broad shoulders and a muscular abdomen beginning to thicken with age. The first brush of gray silvered the light brown hair at his temples, and when he offered Matt a handshake along with a smile, it lit up his forest green eyes.

"It's good to meet you, Matt, is it? Please call me Jorge," her father said with none of the formality he'd sensed from her mother.

"*Sí*, Matt Perez. I'm with SBS," he said as Jorge swept a thickly muscled arm in the direction of the chairs in front of the couch.

"We know SBS well. They handle some of the security for the casino," Raquel said as she returned to the couch, perched herself on the edge of it and smoothed the skirt of her red dress over her knees.

He took a seat and glanced at Teresa, waiting for her to begin. She fidgeted in her seat for a second before she said, "*Mami. Papi.* There's something we need to discuss."

"Is it about your horses?" her mother said with a wrinkle of her nose, disdain dripping from her words.

Jorge reached out and laid a hand over his wife's tightly clasped hands. "Raquel, *por favor.* Let Teresa finish."

Teresa sucked in a rough breath and held it, as if trying to control herself. Clearly mother and daughter had butted heads more than once about the stables.

After releasing a long exhale, Teresa said, "We've had a number of incidents at the stables. That's why Matt and SBS are involved."

She gestured to him with a shaky hand, and he thought it was as good a time as any to jump in and explain. "We've determined that our possible suspect has connections to Tony Hollywood. I assume you're familiar with Hollywood."

Her father blew out a snort. "Familiar? You might say that. We went to the same private school before going our separate ways."

Matt glanced at Teresa, whose hands were gripping the arms of the chair so forcefully her knuckles were white from the pressure. Aware of how difficult this was for her, he couched his words carefully. "When you say you went your separate ways, I assume that means you haven't heard from him in some time."

"We don't work with people like Tony Hollywood," her mother said, face as chilly as the tone of her words.

Matt nodded. "I understand, but does Hollywood want to work with you? Have you had any issues with either him or—"

"Any of his friends?" Jorge said with an arch of a salt-and-pepper eyebrow.

At Matt's nod, her father continued, "You know the mob had quite a lot of influence in many of the casinos in Cuba."

Matt nodded once again and said, "I know the history."

"*Bueno*. What you may not know is our family's history. Both my family and Raquel's owned one of Havana's most well-known casinos. Rumor has it the mob tried to work their way into the business, but our great-grandfathers made it clear—" he raised his fists in emphasis "—that the mob has no place in our casino. We think that message has been well understood over the years."

Matt got his meaning loud and clear but had to press since Teresa's life was at stake. "No recent push—"

"Nothing," Raquel immediately shot back and then glanced at her daughter. "I may not approve of what you do, but we would never ever do anything that could hurt you or your business."

Message received. Again. Pushing to his feet, he peered at the two matching desks and said, "I imagine you both have a lot of work to do."

"We are never too busy for you, *mi'ja*." Jorge slowly rose and held his hand out in the direction of his daughter, who stood, slipped her hand into his and hugged him.

"Gracias, Papi," Teresa said and as she stepped away from him, the bright sheen of tears glimmered in her emerald gaze.

With a sniffle and a brief, stilted hug of her mother, she whirled and hurried to the door.

Matt offered his thanks to her parents and chased after Teresa. As he and Butter caught up to her, he said, "That went...well."

An indifferent shrug was her only answer while they sped through the casino, out through the glass doors and down the steps to the sidewalk, where Teresa finally stopped, bent and sucked in a few rough breaths.

He stroked her back tenderly, gentling the upset that had been caused by the meeting.

When she straightened, she said, "I'm sorry. It's just that...*Mami* and me...she will never forgive my not coming to work for the casino."

Even in just that short meeting he recognized Raquel could be a formidable force and dealing with her could be difficult. "You're following your dream. She should be proud of that."

With a rough breath, she said, "I guess she is. When I

won my first race, she and *Papi* were there, but I got the feeling she had wished we'd lost."

"Her loss," he said and laid a possessive hand at the small of her back. "We should head to the SBS offices and make that call to Esquivel like we decided last night."

"Do you think Sophie and Robbie will be able to trace the call?" she asked as they walked to her car in the nearby parking lot. Although there was a space reserved for her closer to the entrance—probably part of her parents' desire that she come work for them—he had made her park in the general area to avoid attracting attention.

"If he's smart, he's using a burner phone, but we should still be able to check the call detail records to find out where he may be located."

He hopped into the driver's seat and once she was buckled up, he pulled out of the parking lot and drove to Brickell Avenue in downtown Miami, fighting midday traffic. Forty minutes later they had parked and gone up to the upper floors of the building and the SBS offices.

Trey and Mia met them at the front desk.

"Please let Sophie and Robbie know that we need them in the conference room," Trey said to the receptionist, and they all walked into the nearby conference room to wait for them. While they did so, Mia pressed a button by the front door that made the glass wall of the conference room opaque for privacy.

As soon as the Gonzalez cousins had arrived, the meeting began.

"You went to see your parents this morning?" Mia asked. Compassion was evident in her voice and gaze.

"Just now. I had to work one of the horses this morning," Teresa replied and quickly added, "They said they had no connections with Tony Hollywood or anyone else in the mob."

Trey laser focused on Matt. "What was your read?"

With a dip of his head, he said, "I believe them. I don't think they're involved with Hollywood or anyone else. I also think they wouldn't do anything that might hurt Teresa or her business."

"Glad to hear that. If we consider that thread closed, let's move to Finn Walker. Roni's contacts say they're still waiting for the DNA analysis on the cigarette butts, but the fingerprints on the glass confirm he was in your neighbor's house," Trey said.

"Are the fingerprints enough to arrest him?" Teresa asked. She nervously tapped a pen on the notepad in front of her.

"No, not yet, but the noose is tightening." Trey reached out to cover her hand and offer a reassuring squeeze.

"They have an address for Walker, but when they went to question him, the place was vacant," Mia said.

"Do you think we could have the address? I could take Butter to see if she can pick up a scent there," Matt tossed out for consideration.

"We can try to get it. In the meantime, let's reach out to Esquivel. See what he has to say." Trey peered at Sophie and Robbie. "Are you ready to record the conversation?"

Sophie nodded. "We're ready. If he's using the same phone number, we'll have Roni ask the PD to request the call detail records for us to review."

Mia glanced at Teresa. "Are you ready?"

Chapter Twelve

Am I ready? she asked herself. It had taken her the better part of the morning to work up the courage to speak to her parents. She was still shaken by that meeting, but then again that wasn't anything new. Dealing with her mother's disapproval always bothered her.

But she wasn't some wilting wallflower. She could do this and gave a decided nod. "I'm ready."

She pulled out her smartphone and swiped to the voice mail Esquivel had left. Displaying the number, she glanced at the two techies who nodded as one to say they were set. She hit the button for the speakerphone and dialed, holding her breath while it rang and rang.

Over and over the tone sounded, almost echoing in the conference room. She was about to hang up when a breathy voice answered. "Hello?"

"Warner? It's Teresa."

"Teresa, *dios mio.* I've been hoping you'd call," he said, still slightly out of breath as if he was running somewhere.

Trying to stay neutral, she said, "I'm calling. You said this was serious."

"It is, Teresita. *Por favor.* You can't talk to the racing commission. *Por favor,*" he pleaded, and the sounds of traffic drifted across the line. Esquivel was clearly on the move.

"Why shouldn't I? We both know I fired you for using a banned substance on my horse."

"It's about more and it could be dangerous for you," he said, breath choppier.

"Dangerous?" she said, voice rising in anger. "More dangerous than poisoning my horse, shooting at me or trying to run me off the road with an airboat?"

"Deadly…dangerous…believe…me," he said, barely able to talk between his huffing breaths and the noise in the background.

"Why, Warner? Why is it dangerous?" she pressed but Esquivel didn't answer.

A short curse filtered across the line before it went dead.

"Did you get all that?" Trey asked his cousins.

"We did. We'll have Roni get the call detail records for that phone number."

"Can you analyze the sound? Maybe make out where he might be?" Matt asked.

Robbie nodded. "We can try. There was a good deal of background noise. Maybe too much."

"And he was on the run. That was obvious," Trey said, a glower on his handsome face.

"He sounded scared," Teresa added, almost starting to feel a little bit of pity for her former trainer.

"Last time my informant sounded like that he ended up dead," Trey said, and it was obvious that he blamed himself for that.

"Hopefully we can find him before that happens," Matt replied and then faced her. "Can you think of anything besides the doping and banned substances that would warrant having the racing commission involved?"

She sorted through her assorted memories of working with Esquivel, but nothing popped free. "I can't."

"But Esquivel thinks you might have other information. That was clear to me," Mia offered.

Teresa shook her head, unable to disagree but also unable to nail down what Esquivel thought she had on him. "He does, but I can't think of anything."

"And there's Walker in the mix as well. Is he working for Esquivel or Hollywood?" Trey said and doodled something on the pad in front of him where he had written the names of the three suspects.

"Or working alone. What if he's working on his own? What if there's something Teresa has seen that involves only him?" Matt suggested and then glanced at her. "Are you sure you haven't seen Walker before?"

"Could I see a picture of him again?" Teresa asked.

Mia opened a folder sitting in front of her and pulled out Walker's mug shot. She passed it to Trey, who sent it around the table until it reached Teresa.

She laid the photo on the table and scrutinized it. "There's something here, around the eyes," she said and circled an index finger around that area but then shook her head again. "But I just don't remember him. Do you mind if I keep this?"

With a wave of her hand, Mia said, "Go ahead. I can print out another one for the file."

"Gracias," she said and folded the photo in half, intending to look at it again in the hopes of remembering something useful.

TERESA TOOK THE folded photo and fingered it over and over, almost as if that might provide a clue as to what connection she might have to the mobster. When she lifted her gaze and met Matt's, it was clear she was upset with today's developments, and he knew just the thing to make her feel better.

"If there's nothing else, Teresa, Butter and I should get back to the stables," he said.

Trey eyeballed him and then shifted his gaze to Teresa. "Nothing else until we're able to get the call detail records and Sophie and Robbie can analyze the recording."

"Great," he said, and Teresa hopped to her feet beside him, obviously relieved that it was time to go.

"I appreciate all you're doing," she said, ever polite and correct.

The Gonzalez family members all rose from the table and as they walked out, Trey laid a hand on his shoulder and urged him away for a second. Head bent close to his, he said, "Everything okay with you two?"

Matt peered in Teresa's direction as she stood by Mia at the elevator bank, waiting for him. Because he couldn't lie to his friend, he said, "Tense at times. Confusing."

Trey tracked Matt's gaze as he remained focused on the intriguing stables owner. With a nod, his friend said, "I get it, Matt. Just be careful. There's a lot at stake."

"I know," he said and hurried away from Trey to the women, who had been speaking softly while they waited. As he approached, a slight flush of color painted Teresa's cheeks, making him wish he could have been a fly on the wall to hear what they'd been discussing.

"Everything okay?" he asked and clasped his hands in front of him to keep from touching Teresa, afraid that Mia would read way too much from that action.

"We're good," Teresa said and then hugged Mia. "Please keep us posted."

"We will and don't worry. Progress may be slow, but there is progress," Mia said and walked over to call the elevator to the floor.

The door opened barely seconds later and Teresa, Butter

and Matt hurried in for the ride down to the lobby. Uneasy silence filled the space until they reached the ground floor and he asked, "Do you mind if I walk Butter for a bit?"

"Not at all. She's been such a good girl," Teresa said and went to pet the dog, but then pulled back, recalling that she was a working K-9.

He wanted to say it was okay, but he had to keep that separation between work and anything personal for Butter. Especially since he'd failed spectacularly at maintaining that separation himself.

"She is a good girl," he said and rewarded Butter with an ear rub and a treat he had tucked into the pocket of his khakis earlier that morning.

On the sidewalk outside the building, he gave Butter a longer leash so she could explore and relieve herself while Teresa and he slowly strolled a few feet away.

As they walked, Teresa said, "Have you had her for long?"

"Six months give or take, so we're still learning to work together," Matt said with a slight lift of his shoulders and a quick glance all around to make sure it was safe.

With a side-glance at him, she said, "Is that how long you've been with SBS?"

He nodded. "It is. Before that I was with Miami Beach PD's K-9 unit."

From his peripheral vision, he noticed Butter squatting by a nearby streetlight pole and stopped to let her relieve herself. As he did so, he swept his gaze all across the plaza in front of the building. Satisfied all was secure, he focused on Teresa.

A mistake. Big mistake.

She'd dressed up more today, probably in deference to the visit to her parents. A pale yellow sundress bared her shoulders and arms that had a slight T-shirt tan thanks to her work with the horses. The lemony color accented that tan and the deep jewel-like color of her eyes.

A soft bark jerked his attention to Butter. The shepherd had taken a spot right next to Teresa and was gazing up at him as if to ask, *What's up?*

He coughed to release the pressure that had built in his gut at the sight of Teresa and blurted out, "We should head back. I know you have work to do."

"I do. I need to see if Frijoles is up for some exercise," she said, and they quickly walked to her car. When they slipped inside and he started the short drive back to stables, he said, "Frijoles is important to you."

His statement was more of a question, wanting an answer she wasn't sure she was ready to give. But he'd shared a little bit about himself just minutes earlier and so she shared as well.

"He's my best stallion. His stud fees will help immensely and I'm hoping that when his foal is born, it will be a winner as well."

"His foal? Is that the one Ay Caramba is carrying?" Matt asked with a quick glance in her direction.

"It is. He'll be a dad any day now," she said, joy filling her at the thought of the foal's birth and training it for the future.

"And we'll make sure he and his horse family will be okay," Matt assured her.

"Horse family?" She laughed, prompting a chuckle from Matt.

"Yes, horse family. Just like your family," he said.

He surprised her with the sudden shift to something not necessarily as happy as the coming birth of the foal. He cast a quick, uneasy look in her direction and said, "I'm sorry. I know I've hit a nerve."

"You could say that," she said with a harsh laugh.

"Your mom—"

"My *mami* and me is…complicated." She shook her head before plowing on. "I know she loves me and wants the best for me."

"Sounds like you're trying to convince yourself of that," Matt said, ever observant. While the first meeting had been awkward, in the days since then she'd come to realize there was a lot more to him than just his handsome face and all that tempting muscle.

"I know she loves me, but ever since I took a bad fall a few years ago, she's been determined to have me join the family business," she admitted, surprised at herself for confiding in him.

He must've realized she'd said more than she'd intended to, so he apparently decided to share a memory that was more personal than anything he'd revealed before.

"I get it. When I started playing football, I think my mom wanted to package me in bubble wrap to keep me safe when I took a hit," he said with a laugh.

She smiled and joined in his laughter. "I guess moms just want to keep us safe."

With a grin as he pulled off the road that led to the stables, he said, "Just like you want to keep Frijoles and his horse family safe."

His infectious grin and the laughter in his voice yanked another chuckle from her. "Just like that," she said and added in a slightly more thoughtful tone, "Just like you want to keep us safe."

"It's my…job," he said, but his hesitation made it obvious that it was about more than that for him. A burst of warmth flared to life inside her chest, bringing comfort and unexpected hope. She didn't want to think about what she was hoping for.

Unsure of what to say, she opted for, "I appreciate all that you're doing."

His answer was a short grunt, and luckily, he was already turning into the driveaway for the stables. When he parked the car in front of the house, he said, "I'm going to patrol the grounds. See if the guards have anything to say."

With a quick bop of her head, she said, "I'll go work Frijoles."

TERESA DASHED FROM the car and as she did so, Butter gave a little bark, clearly disquieted by her departure.

Matt half turned in the seat and rubbed Butter's ears. "She'll be okay, girl. Frijoles wouldn't hurt her," he said, recalling the friskier horse she'd tamed days before. Not that an accident couldn't happen while she was training. Even though he didn't normally follow horse racing, he'd seen news reports about the death of a horse or jockey during a race.

But Teresa could take care of herself on a horse, he thought, although he planned on doing some research to find out more about the fall that had freaked out her mother.

Exiting the car, he freed Butter from the harness securing her in the back seat and walked her to the ATV for their patrol. Not wanting to disturb Teresa's workout on the track, he patrolled the driveway first, checking in with the guard at the gate who had been instructed to keep an eye out for any activity at the neighbor's house.

Nothing, so he pressed on, moving slowly along the perimeter of the grounds, vigilant for signs of any activity or changes that would say someone had been there. He stopped at the second guard who had nothing to report, and then finally moved toward the track and the last guard on duty. But as he neared the track there was no sign of Teresa, Richard or Frijoles.

His chest tightened with pressure and the sudden pounding of his heartbeat in his ears almost deafened him. Finishing the route, he rushed back to park by the stables. When he did so, Butter grew agitated and began pawing the seat beside him.

"What's wrong, Butter? Find it," he said, and the shepherd took off in the direction of the stables entrance.

Chapter Thirteen

Gun drawn, Matt raced after his dog, who had gone to the open door of Ay Caramba's stall. Teresa's trainer, Richard, stood there, hands on his hips as he watched what was happening inside. Butter was at his feet, pacing back and forth across the opening, obviously agitated.

Matt joined them. Teresa was inside the stall at Ay Caramba's head, calming the horse while Dr. Ramirez had her hands inside the mare. Luis stood by with a handful of towels.

"The foal's position is a little off. Miranda has to shift his legs," Richard whispered, and Matt holstered his weapon.

"Got it!" Miranda called out. When she pulled her hands out, she was holding two spindly legs covered by a thin white sack.

Miranda leaned back. The horse's sides heaved, and more of the legs and sack became visible as well as...

Was that a nose? Matt thought and suddenly there was a head.

The sack split open and dangled downward, revealing the foal.

Miranda pulled on the legs as the mare pushed, and Teresa tried to calm the horse, who had begun to prance.

"Easy, girl. You're going to be a mom soon," Teresa crooned.

Another push and the foal's body emerged. Miranda cradled the horse and Richard rushed forward to stand by Teresa. "You should help Miranda," he said.

Teresa kneeled by Miranda to assist, and with another push, the rest of the foal and sack spilled from the mare.

Miranda and Teresa cradled the foal and moved it away from Ay Caramba's hooves, the remnants of the sack trailing from the foal to its mother. Teresa cleared away the sack from the foal's face and body and then the vet and Teresa gently laid the foal on the ground. For long seconds the foal was motionless.

Matt sucked in a breath and held it, waiting for any motion that said the foal was alive, but nothing happened immediately.

Miranda grabbed a handful of straw and whisked it across the foal's nose and the baby abruptly reared its head and sat up.

"That's it. That's a good boy," Teresa said and tenderly ran a hand across the foal's side, pulling away the remnants of the amniotic sack. Matt realized that the foal was still connected to the mother with the umbilical cord.

Recalling how EMTs had dealt with pregnant mothers, he gestured to the cord. "Don't you have to cut that?"

Teresa grabbed a towel from Luis and wiped her hands clean as she walked to Matt and Butter's side. Butter had calmed down and sat by his side, intensely watching the foal.

Shaking her head, Teresa said, "Not in horses. There's still blood flowing from the mother to the foal that's essential. If it doesn't come off naturally, we'll cut it off once the flow stops."

Ay Caramba walked closer to the foal, dipped her head and nudged her baby, who shifted his head to look up at his mother.

"It may take the foal several minutes to try to get to its feet," Miranda said as she rose from beside the foal and slipped off the long surgical gloves she was wearing. Turning them inside out, she tossed them into her medical bag and grabbed the bag.

Richard and Miranda walked to the entrance to the stall and waved at Luis to join them.

"We should give them a little alone time so we don't stress them out," Miranda explained. "It could be a couple of hours for the foal to start to nurse and also for the afterbirth." She ran a hand across Richard's arm. "Unless something seems out of the ordinary, I'll be back tomorrow to check on them."

"Thank you for everything, Miranda. I know you must be exhausted," Teresa said and went to hug the older woman but paused since they were both wet and dirty from the birth.

"A little tired but so happy to see them both healthy," the veterinarian said with a full-lipped smile.

"I'll walk you to your car," Richard said, laying a hand at the small of her back, and the two strolled out, heads bent toward each other, chatting.

"Is there anything else we need to do?" Matt asked, unfamiliar with what happened during the entire foaling process.

"We should leave them alone for a little bit. You have eyes on this area, right?" she asked.

Matt nodded. "I do."

"Great. Luis, it's okay for you to go home and get some rest. Matt and I can keep an eye on them."

"Hasta mañana," Luis said with a wave and walked to the far end of the stables and the nearby bunkhouse.

"Hasta mañana," Matt and Teresa replied in unison.

"If you don't mind, I'd like to get cleaned up," Teresa said. She snagged a towel from the pile Luis had brought out of the stall and wiped her hands again, leaving dirty streaks on the cloth.

"Not at all. I need to do some things before dinner," he said, ignoring the fact that even covered in who knew what had come out of the horse, she was still the most beautiful woman he'd ever seen.

They hurried to the house, where Teresa went upstairs and he raced to the monitors, intent on checking things out, but also to research something that had been bouncing around in his head since their drive back to the stables.

With Butter settling in beside him, he took a quick look at the screens. Nothing seemed out of order. If anything, it tugged at his heart to see the foal awkwardly find its footing and approach its mother. Ay Caramba bent her head and nuzzled her baby, almost protectively.

Matt understood that protectiveness. His mom had been fierce and always in his corner.

Much like Teresa's mom seemed to be, despite her misguided, passive-aggressive behavior.

Sitting down at the computer, he typed in Teresa's name and pulled up a few articles about her fall. It hit him then why her mother had such fear about what Teresa was doing. Teresa had taken a freak spill during a dressage event when her horse spooked and threw her. She'd broken her back so badly the doctors had feared she might be paralyzed. Her miraculous recovery had surprised them, but it had taken over a year for her to return to riding.

He sat back in his chair, a whirlpool of emotions swirling through him. Shock. Worry. Pride. Respect.

"She's quite a woman," he said to Butter, who sat up, a puzzled look on her face. Bending to massage her neck and rub her ears, he said, "It's okay, girl."

Only it really wasn't, he thought. With everything he

learned about Teresa, it was harder and harder to ignore what an amazing woman she was. Harder to deny that she intrigued him. Made him want her in ways he hadn't wanted a woman in way too long.

Sucking in a breath to fight back that need, he took a last look at the monitors. Satisfied that all was well, he texted Sophie and Robbie to set up a schedule for them to take over the surveillance. When they sent back a time, he thanked them and headed to the kitchen, where Teresa was pulling things out of the fridge to make dinner.

"How can I help?" he asked.

"I'm just going to make some picadillo. Is that okay?" she said as she laid a package of ground beef on the counter. There was already a pot on the stove, probably rice cooking.

"I love picadillo. My mom used to make it for me a lot." The simple dish of seasoned ground beef was comfort food at its best and inexpensive. Plus, leftovers could be used to fill empanadas or tacos.

"What was she like, your mom?" Teresa asked as she cut up some peppers, onions and garlic.

"My *mami* was…amazing," he said and since Teresa had the meal under control, he set the table and then joined her by the stove, where she had tossed the vegetables into a skillet with olive oil. It took only a few seconds for the aroma of the frying vegetables to spice the air.

Teresa stirred them and then looked up at him as she said, "You miss her."

Since there was no denying it, he said, "I do. She always believed in me."

TERESA HEARD WHAT was there beneath the words: his mother had believed in him when no one else had.

"Moms…it can be complicated," she said and placed the

ground beef in with the vegetables, using her wooden spoon to break up the pieces as the meat browned. She turned down the heat on the pot of rice as the water started to boil.

"It's hard to sit back when someone you love could be hurt."

The tone in his voice yanked her gaze from the skillet up to meet his blue-eyed gaze. There was worry there and she tried to dispel it.

"I know what I'm doing," she said, returning her attention to the meat in the pan.

"Accidents happen when we least expect them, don't they?"

The words hung in the air, and she tried to ignore them, plucking capers and olives from their bottles to add to the skillet. She opened a can and poured tomato sauce into the skillet before adding a few raisins and seasoning the mix with cumin, oregano, salt and black pepper.

"Teresa?" he pressed at her prolonged silence.

"It was a freak accident," she said, realizing that he had done some homework since their morning meeting with her parents.

"But you get why she worries. You were almost paralyzed," he said and reached for the cover on the rice, but she playfully swatted his hand back.

"You have to let it steam so it's fluffy," she explained.

"Got it," he said and laid his arms across his chest, drawing her attention there. Reminding her of what it felt like to be held in those arms. Of that hard chest beneath her cheek, heart beating loudly for her. So tempting, but before she gave in to that temptation—again—she wanted to know more about what had shaped him. Especially since he'd obviously delved into her past.

"You hardly mention your dad," she said, giving the picadillo a stir.

He shrugged his broad shoulders. "Not much to mention."

"You had a good relationship with him?"

Another shrug was his reply, but that wasn't going to cut it with her. "Come on, Matt. You obviously know my deepest, darkest—"

"He wasn't there for me," he blurted out and shook his head, the motion so strong it sent the unruly waves of his hair shifting back and forth. In a softer voice, he said, "When I needed him the most, he didn't have my back."

Sensing his upset, she laid a hand on his shoulder and stroked it gently. "I'm sorry."

"Don't be. I learned my mistake," he said, words curt and filled with pain.

Pressing him might bring more pain, but it was like pulling off a bandage. It hurt when you did it but then felt way better.

"What was the mistake?" She shifted her hand up to cradle his jaw.

His muscles jumped beneath her palm as he said, "I dared to fly too close to the sun."

IT SHOCKED HIM to admit that, but he knew she wouldn't be satisfied unless she knew the whole story.

"I played football in high school. Good enough that I got a scholarship to a division one college, only… I dared to get involved with girl who was way out of my league." The memories came so fast and furious he had to stop and take a long breath to hold back the emotions they aroused.

"She was the sun," Teresa said and stroked a thumb across his cheek, the simple gesture comforting.

"Her daddy didn't like that she was involved with someone who was literally from the wrong side of the tracks. He went to the cops and said I'd forced myself on her and that's all it took. When word spread, I became an outcast in town and the college pulled my scholarship."

"But you didn't do it. Didn't the police investigate? Didn't your father stand up for you?"

He was grateful she trusted him enough to know it had all been a lie. What he wouldn't have given for more people like her when he'd been eighteen and fighting the system alone.

"My dad was either too afraid or too drunk to back me up. As for the police, they cleared me, but the damage was done. I tried to get my scholarship back, but the coach said they couldn't risk the bad publicity."

He laid his hand on hers and gently turned it to take her hand into his. "*Gracias* for believing in me."

"I have no reason to doubt you. You've always been truthful. You did call me smelly the first time we met," she said with a cute wrinkle of her nose.

"I'm sorry I did that. I was in rich girl denial mode because you were…" he began, but then stopped and muttered a curse. Shaking his head, he locked his gaze on hers and finally admitted what he'd been fighting since first laying eyes on her. "You were—you are—the sun."

DIOS, BUT THAT was way more than what she'd expected him to say. Worse, she liked it way too much. Liked him way too much.

She leaned into him and went up on tiptoes until her lips were barely an inch from his and his warm rough breath spilled against hers. "My parents are rich. I'm just a girl with some horses," she whispered and closed that final distance to kiss him.

He groaned at that first contact and stiffened, but as

she kept on kissing him, her mouth mobile against his, he finally wrapped an arm around her waist and hauled her close. Over and over they kissed until the slight crackle from the stove and slightly toasty smell had them pulling apart.

Teresa shut the gas on the pot with the rice and whipped off the cover. "It's overcooked."

Matt leaned closer to the pot and peered inside. "I like the *raspas*. Those hard bits at the bottom are tasty."

He was being overly kind, although her *papi* had always teased her *mami* that he liked the toasty rice as well on the rare occasions when her mother cooked and messed up.

"We should eat. I have to check on Ay Caramba and her foal," she said and quickly served up the picadillo and rice.

As she laid the plates on the table, Matt held up his smartphone to show her the camera feed in the stables. Mama and baby seemed to be doing fine, but she was still itching to see them.

They finished their meal quickly. While she was loading the dishwasher, Matt gave Butter a fresh bowl of water and food. The dog gobbled up the kibble quickly, almost as if she was as eager as Teresa to go see the new baby.

Back in the stables, they headed straight to Ay Caramba's stall where the foal was nursing, and the mare had apparently passed the afterbirth without any issues. Teresa carefully scooped it up in case the vet wanted to see it, mindful that new mothers could be overprotective and possibly dangerous.

"They're both doing fine." She closed the door to the stall, nudging Butter out of the way since the dog was intently watching.

"I'm always surprised at how animals seem to know there's a baby around," she said as Matt demanded Butter's attention with a hand signal.

They strolled to Frijoles's stall and the bay walked up to the door and stuck his head over the edge. There was something almost excited about the way he tossed his head and did a little prance. She smiled, stroked his nose and said, "Yes, you did good. Your baby is beautiful."

The horse huffed out a breath as if to say, *I sure did.*

Matt hesitantly reached out to likewise rub the horse's nose, and after he did so, he held his hand out to Teresa and she slipped her hand into his.

Together, they finished a look around the stables and then headed outside to the ATV. Matt didn't need to ask if she wanted to go with him. She eased into the passenger seat while he loaded Butter into the storage box.

He started up the ATV and they did a run around the perimeter of the property, checking in with the various guards stationed there. Luckily there was nothing to report.

Matt detoured to go around the track and the rear of the stables and she enjoyed the quiet of the coming night. In what seemed like too short a ride, they were back at the house. After taking Butter for a walk so she could relieve herself, they headed inside, but at the door they hesitated, awkwardness creeping in.

Matt jerked a thumb in the direction of the dining room. "I should get to work."

Not that he hadn't been working during the drive, but she got what he meant. Being together on the drive and during their dinner had felt like anything but work. But she was reluctant for their night together to end.

"I can make some coffee if you'd like."

A broad smile lit up his face and turned his blue eyes to a jewel-like sapphire. "I'd like that."

He dropped a quick kiss on her cheek, whirled and rushed to the dining room.

Chapter Fourteen

Matt braced his hands on the tabletop and peered intently at the various monitors.

All was peaceful, especially in the stables where Ay Caramba and her foal had lain down, the baby tucked tight to her mother.

The whir of the grinder in the coffee machine rang through the house, distracting him for a second. But then he returned to perusing the monitors, wanting to make sure that the area was secure. That Teresa and her horses were safe.

Satisfied, he sat down at the computer and checked his email for updates from his colleagues at SBS. An email had just come in from Sophie and Robbie. He opened the analysis of the call detail records for Esquivel and the report on the tape recording.

He had barely opened the attachments with the analysis when his phone rang. Trey was calling.

"Hola, jefe," he teased since Trey wasn't a fan of anyone calling him "Chief."

A bark of a laugh burst across the line before Trey said, "Very funny. How's it going?"

"All is good here."

"I didn't want to push with Teresa there, but what was your read of her parents?" Trey asked just as Teresa came in with two mugs of steaming coffee.

Matt shot her an uneasy look, but then forged ahead. "The Rodriguezes insist that Walker or Hollywood have no connection to their casino."

"Do you believe them?" Trey pressed.

Teresa sat beside him and placed the mug before him with a shaky hand, obviously aware of what they were discussing.

Matt met her gaze as he said, "I believe them. I don't think there's any connection to the casino."

He was therefore surprised when Trey said, "The analysis of the cell phone data and recording says the contrary. Why don't you look at the reports, talk to Teresa and call me back."

The line went dead, and he put the phone down on the table and faced Teresa, who had overheard bits and pieces of the conversation.

"It has nothing to do with my parents."

He laid his hand on hers as she cupped the mug, as if she needed the heat to chase away an inner chill.

"I believe you and them, but we have data that says otherwise." He released her hands, returned to the keyboard and brought up Sophie and Robbie's analysis.

He hadn't done much work with call detail records, but his SBS team had made it easy to see what had led Trey to his conclusion. With a finger, Matt explained the first page of data to Teresa.

"These are the numbers Esquivel has called as well as the switches and cell sites that picked up the call," he said and then flipped to the next page of the report. "Sophie and Robbie plotted that information on a map."

Teresa's sharp, surprised exhale cut through the air. "Those locations are all near the casino."

Matt nodded and pulled up the SBS report on the voice recording. Sophie and Robbie had peeled away Esquivel's voice to isolate key noises in the background and identify what they were. They had embedded those noises in the report and Matt clicked on one to play it.

What sounded like a whir was followed by a few electronic tones, another louder whir and then coins dropping into a bucket.

"That sounds like a slot machine," Teresa said, defeat clear in her voice.

Matt wasn't about to accept the results so quickly. As a cop, he'd more than once come across cases that seemed clear-cut but weren't.

"Is there another reason why Esquivel would be in this area? Family maybe?"

With a slow shake of her head, she said, "As far as I know, most of his family is in the Little Havana area."

Matt nodded and pressed on. "Any other gambling locations in the area?"

Teresa tipped her head from side to side and then said, "There are a few places in and around the casino that try to glom business."

"Would they have slot machines?"

"Probably. They're cheaper than gaming tables with dealers."

"I'll head there—"

"*We'll* head there," she immediately corrected.

Matt smiled, nodded and cupped her cheek. "We'll head there as soon as you've finished your morning chores."

"*Gracias.* You don't know what it means to me that you're willing to trust me that it has nothing to do with my parents," she said, and a small smile slipped onto her features.

The pat response would have been to say that he was only doing his job, but in just a few short days Teresa had become much more than that.

"I do know. I know your parents are important to you and I believe them, and you, when you say it has nothing to do with the casino. But if it doesn't—"

"Why are Walker and Hollywood involved with Esquivel?" she finished for him. "I get it."

With a few quick taps on the keyboard, Matt pulled up Walker's mug shot. "You say he doesn't seem familiar."

TERESA LEANED FORWARD and focused on the photo, looking at every aspect of his face. A weasel-like face, narrow with a pointy nose and long chin. Unfamiliar except for the eyes. Crystal-blue eyes, cold as ice.

"His eyes," she said and circled a finger in their general direction. "They seem familiar but the rest of his face… It's too…skinny," she said and motioned to her own face to better explain what she meant.

"If his face was fuller?" He grabbed a drawing tablet and pen from the tabletop and manipulated the image to make Walker's cheeks and jaw broader.

As he did so, something clicked in her brain. "Can you put a full beard on him? Make his hair darker? Longer?"

With the pen, Matt drew in a beard in a darker brown, colored in his hair and lengthened it. When he did so, Teresa gasped. "I think I've seen him. With Esquivel and more than once."

"Where?" Matt asked and saved the photo.

Teresa peered at the image and then screwed her eyes shut, trying to recall. With a shake of her head, she said, "Three or four times at different racetracks. He was working in the stable areas."

"Is it possible he was involved with the doping?" Matt asked.

She nodded. "It's possible. If what I'm remembering is right, he had access to administer the drugs."

"That's probably another reason the racing commission wants to speak to you," Matt said and closed the photo.

"Maybe it's time we spoke to the representative for the commission. Find out what it really is that they want from me," she said and finally took a sip of her coffee.

"I agree. If the racing commission has put Esquivel and Walker together, we'll know it has nothing to do with the casino," Matt said, and she didn't miss the worry in his voice.

"But we won't know what Hollywood has to do with this," she said, aware of the reasons for his concern.

"We won't, but if Hollywood is involved, we will figure out how to protect you," he said, cradling her cheek. He stroked it with his thumb and then dropped it down to lovingly trace the edges of her lips.

That touch, gentle and full of tenderness, reached deep inside, igniting the need for his touch, but also for him. For the man he was, strong and caring.

Leaning forward, she brushed her lips across his and invited him to join her.

A rough breath exploded from him as he said, "This is crazy." But even though he said it, he met her lips with his, accepting her invitation. Driving his hand into her hair to hold her close as they kissed, breaths melding. The kiss deepening as she opened her mouth and tasted him.

Her moan split the air, stunning her with the need in that simple sound.

HER BODY JUMPED beside his and he sensed the surprise there and tempered his kiss.

Shifting away from her, he met her emerald gaze, nearly

black with desire, and ran his thumb across her lips, moist from his kisses.

"We need to take this slow."

A sexy and yet also innocent smile slipped onto her lips. "Slow is always better."

Already hard with passion, he almost forgot his responsibilities, tempted to take her upstairs and show her just how slow and good it could be. But he was a man who recognized duty and honor, and that made him temper his hunger.

"I want you, Teresa. I can't deny that, but not until I know you're safe."

Her smile dimmed but didn't harden with his words. "I knew you'd say that, and it only proves to me why you're a special kind of man."

Special. It had been way too long since he'd felt that way. Not since he was a teen and his mother had been alive. Not since the debacle that had cost him his future as a college football player and had driven him onto an unknown path that had led him here. To her.

"I'll walk you to your room so I can get back to work," he said, needing space from her to focus on what was happening on the monitors and also to advise Trey that Teresa had been able to identify Walker.

He rose and held his hand out to her, and she slipped her hand into his. With his free hand he commanded Butter to follow them up to the door of Teresa's room. At her door, he dropped a quick kiss on her cheek, not trusting himself to do more.

"Get some sleep. We're going to have a busy day tomorrow."

"I'll try. You get some rest also," she said, brushed a fleeting kiss across his lips and closed her door.

Matt waited there for a heartbeat before hurrying back

to the dining room with Butter at his side. He shut the door, needing privacy, and dialed Trey as Butter sat at his feet.

"You finished reviewing the reports?" Trey immediately asked. The sounds of a television filtered across the line until Roni apparently muted it.

"We did and yes, the locations from the calls are near the casino, but not at it." Matt sat down and pulled up the information again.

"What about the background noises that Sophie and Robbie isolated? It sounded like a slot machine to me," Trey countered, clearly convinced that the attacks on Teresa had more to do with the casino than whatever the racing commission was investigating.

Matt was determined to convince him otherwise. "I agree, but Teresa says there are locations in and around the casino that also have gaming. Plus, after we played around with the mug shot and gave Walker a beard, something clicked with Teresa."

"Meaning?" Trey pressed.

"She thought she saw Finn Walker at a couple of different racetracks. It's possible he was working with Esquivel to dope the horses," Matt explained and then pushed on. "I think we need to talk to the racing commission as soon as possible to see what they want with Teresa."

He heard the muffled sounds of Trey and Roni chatting but couldn't make out what they were saying. A minute later, Trey said, "We can arrange that. Anything else?"

"Once Teresa finishes working the horses in the morning, we're going to check out those locations around the casino," he said.

Muffled voices came again before Trey said, "Roni said to be careful. If Hollywood is involved, it could be very dangerous. We've already reached out to our contacts over at the Organized Crime division to see if they've heard anything."

"Keep me posted."

"Will do. Try to get some rest," Trey said and ended the call.

Matt laid his phone down on the table and focused his attention on the report that had the locations of Esquivel's calls, pinpointing the addresses. Satisfied with the list he compiled, he perused the monitors again. There was no activity, so he rose and called for Butter to follow him with a low whistle.

The shepherd padded beside him as he walked out of the house and toward the stables. Teresa's horses were more than just her business. They were a piece of her heart and he wanted to make sure they were all safe and sound.

In Ay Caramba's stall, the spindly-legged foal was still next to his mother but awake and nursing. The sight brought unexpected joy and peace through him. He pressed on to Frijoles, who was asleep in his stall as were many of the other horses as he made a round of the stables.

Satisfied all was in order, he did a quick stroll around the perimeter of the building, and after, circled the house and walked to the pond. From there the guard at the entrance to the property was visible, doing his own rounds along the road.

Matt watched, waiting until the guard had returned to his vehicle before walking Butter along the edges of the driveway so she could relieve herself for the night.

At the front door, he rubbed her ears and gave her a treat. "You're a good girl."

She jumped up on his shoulders and licked his face before settling down at his feet as he stood on the porch, surveying the property for one last time before going back into the house.

Locking the front door, he unleashed Butter and said, "Stay, girl. Stay. No one comes in without you barking. Got it?"

The dog licked his face again before circling around and around and lying down across the floor before the front door.

"Good girl," he said once more, left a treat by her nose and then headed to the dining room.

All was peaceful for the moment, but if Hollywood was involved in whatever was going on, that peace wasn't going to last for long.

Because of that, he pulled up all the reports again to review them. Then he searched the internet for anything he could find about the ruthless mobster. Article after article came up about his various crimes, including the possible murder of a casino owner nearly a decade earlier. Despite all the allegations, the police and FBI hadn't been able to secure enough evidence to charge Tony Hollywood with any of the crimes.

Which only made him even more determined to keep Teresa from becoming another of Hollywood's victims. Armed with that determination, he worked through the night to prepare for the next day. Promptly at five as agreed, Sophie came on board so he could get a few hours of sleep.

Softly he tiptoed out of the room and toward the front door.

It was dark in the room, as the sun had yet to come up. Butter was still on guard. As he approached, she rose to her feet and turned in his direction, ready for action.

"Easy, girl," he whispered, and at that, the shepherd dropped to the ground once more.

He tiptoed up the stairs, careful to bypass the third step since he'd noticed that it creaked, and he didn't want to wake Teresa.

At her door he paused. Listened. Nothing.

He was about to keep on going when the door to her room suddenly flew open and Teresa stood there, wearing nothing but an oversize cotton T-shirt.

Chapter Fifteen

She shouldn't have opened the door, but she hadn't really been sleeping. The soft tread of his footsteps had drawn her and now there she was. Now there *he* was.

His hair was rumpled, as if he'd run his hand one too many times through the thick waves. A barely-there smudge beneath his eyes, like charcoal on a drawing, highlighted their intense blue. Lines of tension bracketed his mouth until he saw her, and a soft smile inched across his lips.

"Buenos dias," he said and leaned a forearm on the doorjamb, pulling his polo shirt tight against the hard muscles of his chest.

"Buenos dias, although the sun isn't up yet." She flicked a hand in the direction of her window and the darkness outside.

"More reason both of us should get in bed and get some sleep," he said, shifting away from the door.

"Matt," she said and laid a hand on his arm to stop him. "Please don't leave me. I don't want to be alone."

He blew out a tortured breath and drove a hand through his hair. "If I stay, neither of us is going to get much sleep."

She held her hands up in a surrender gesture. "I promise I'll keep my hands to myself."

A wry twist of his lips advised that he either didn't believe her or if he did, he wanted it to be different. But neither kept him from stepping through her door, taking her hand and walking to her bed.

She climbed back in as he toed off his shoes and lay down on her bed as close to the edge as he could.

As she inched next to him, it was impossible to miss the stiffness in his body. She smoothed a hand across his chest. "Relax. You'll never get any sleep if you don't relax."

LIKE HE COULD relax with her luscious curves pressed into his side and the tease of her silky hair along the underside of his jaw. As she shifted to settle even closer to him, the movement roused a flowery scent from the strands. *Jasmine, maybe?*

"You smell good," he murmured.

A carefree laugh burst from her, and she leaned her head on her elbow to gaze at him. "Not horse smell, huh? You never did apologize for that."

"Can't handle the truth?" he teased and urged her head back down against his chest because otherwise he would be too tempted to kiss those smiling lips.

"Mmm," she hummed and soothed her hand across his chest again. "Truth is, I'm not happy about what's happening in my life, but I'm glad it brought us together."

Together. That word ricocheted in his head over and over as he lay there, fighting the urge to kiss her. Fighting the desire to turn and cover her body with his. Slip that thin layer of cotton off her and explore all that smooth, lush skin.

"Relax," she said again, sensing the tension that had escalated with his thoughts.

He inhaled deeply, counted to ten and slowly released his breath, willing his body to soften. Forcing any thoughts of what he wanted to do with her from his brain. Repeating that long inhale in, exhale out, until he finally found some peacefulness.

When a soft snore spilled from her lips, he smiled and finally let slumber claim him.

THE DIM SOUND of Matt's phone alarm warned that he'd be up and about soon.

She heard her door open, and minutes later the whoosh of water through the pipes as he showered.

While some bacon was frying, she slipped bread into the toaster oven and turned it on. Melting butter in a skillet, she beat a few eggs and spilled them into the skillet.

She had just finished scrambling the eggs when Matt came into the kitchen, Butter trailing behind him.

"Buenos dias. Otra vez," she teased, reminding him that they'd already wished each other a good morning.

He sauntered over, laid a hand on her waist and whispered against her lips, "You're a woman of your word."

He kissed her, leaving her no doubt that he wished she'd broken her promise to keep her hands to herself.

She opened her mouth on his, returning his kiss, and letting him know that she wished she'd broken her promise as well.

They drifted apart, breathing heavily. The smell of toast and bacon, and the shrill sound of Matt's phone ringing reminded them that their lives were not their own and passion would have to wait.

Matt whirled from her and answered his phone. After a second, he said, "Let me put you on speaker."

He walked back to her side and held the phone up between them while Butter took a position at his feet, head cocked as if ready to listen as well. "Go ahead, Mia."

"Trey and I called the representative for the racing commission and after explaining what was happening, we convinced them to reschedule the interview. There's just one thing," Mia said.

"What is it?" Teresa asked, wondering what was putting such uncertainty in her friend's voice.

"He's insisting on having the interview in person," Mia explained.

"When will he be able to get here?" Matt asked, clearly worried about any delay.

"Tomorrow. We arranged for him to come to the SBS offices. Is two o'clock good?" Mia asked.

It would interfere with the training she'd had planned for her client's skittish horse, but finding out what the racing commission was investigating could help put an end to the threats to her life and the stables.

"Whatever you need. I'll be there," she said.

"Great. Also, Roni thinks we may have the DNA results today. We'll keep you posted when they come in," Mia said.

Matt and Teresa shared a look and Matt said, "Teresa and I are going to check out those locations around the casino later. We'll let you know what we find out."

"*Gracias*. Be careful out there," Mia said and ended the call.

Matt was about to put away his phone when she laid a wobbly hand on his to stop him. "Do you think the DNA will prove it's Walker?"

"I think so," he said with no hesitation.

Fear tightened her gut and made her hand even shakier against his. She looked down, avoiding Matt's gaze. He dipped his head and put himself in her line of sight, making it impossible for her to avoid his gaze.

"You're worried that it'll be him because of your parents?"

She pursed her lips, afraid to admit it. Afraid that if it was Walker, it meant Hollywood might be involved.

Matt cupped her jaw and gently urged her head upward to meet his gaze directly. "Whatever the DNA says, we will deal with it."

With a curt bob of her head, she said, "Let's eat before it gets cold."

IT DIDN'T TAKE a genius to see Teresa was upset, so he didn't press. He followed her into the kitchen, and she spooned out eggs and forked bacon onto the plates. He gingerly plucked the toast from the toaster oven, fingers burning as he placed them on a dish.

He laid the dish on the table between the place settings and returned to the counter to pour himself some coffee and freshen her cup. Grabbing both coffees, he placed them on the table. Then he refilled Butter's water bowl and scooped out food for her.

Butter gobbled down the kibble quickly and looked up at him as if waiting for more. "Are you hungry, girl?" he said and affectionately rubbed her ears. Feeling guilty since she'd spent the night guarding the front door instead of with him as she usually did, he fed her a treat as well.

She followed him to the table and lay down beside him as they sat to eat.

Breakfast was relatively silent, with the barest exchange of words about how good the eggs were and how he liked his bacon crispy. He didn't press, aware of her fears and knowing that talking about it right now would do little to alleviate them.

But he was sure her horses and work would help and the sooner she got to the stables, the quicker she'd feel better. Because of that, he made short work of his meal, and she did as well. Together they cleaned off the table, got everything in the dishwasher and were off to the stables in barely minutes.

When they arrived, Richard and Miranda were with Ay Caramba and her foal.

"How are they doing?" Teresa asked and leaned by the entrance to the stall. He stood just behind her, and Butter slipped to the open area in the doorway, intently watching the two horses, her quirky tongue hanging out of her mouth.

Miranda's broad smile answered them even before she spoke. "Mama and baby are doing great."

Teresa's body visibly shook as relief swept through her. "That's good to hear."

Richard stroked his hand across the foal's flank and grinned. "He's strong like his papa. I feel it in my bones that he's going to be a winner."

Teresa's full-lipped smile was free of worry and her emerald eyes glittered with joy as she said, "I can't wait to see him run."

"What are you going to name him?" Miranda said and strolled over to where they stood.

Teresa's shoulders dipped up and down and then she looked at Matt. "What was your mom's name?"

Brows furrowed, he asked, "Alejandra. Why?"

That full joyous smile came again. "Let's call him Alejandro after Matt's *mami*."

He was touched and cupped her cheek. "You don't have to."

She caressed her hand with his. "I want to. She was very special to you and this foal is very special to me."

Just as Teresa was very special to him. "*Gracias*. I hope Alejandro will make Papa proud."

"Speaking of Papa, he's doing very well all things considered," Miranda said, walking toward Frijoles's stall.

"Is he up for a workout? An easy one?" Teresa asked.

Miranda nodded and rubbed the horse's nose as Frijoles ambled over to the stall door.

"He is, but a very easy workout. *Verdad*, Frijoles?" Miranda crooned and stroked the horse again.

Frijoles tossed his head excitedly, as if understanding her. With a smile, Miranda said, "My work here is done. I will be back tomorrow to check on Ay Caramba and Alejandro."

"Sounds good and thank you for everything," Teresa said and hugged the other woman hard, holding the embrace for a long moment.

"*De nada*, Teresita. I know how important they are to you," the older woman said and shot him a look over Teresa's shoulder, as if to say, *"She's important to me."*

"*Gracias*, Miranda," he said with a slow dip of his head to let the older woman know he understood her concern.

The vet nodded, stepped away from Teresa and walked to where Richard waited by Ay Caramba's stall. Together, Miranda and Richard strolled to the car.

"Can you help me saddle him up?" Teresa asked Matt but didn't wait for his answer to hand him Frijoles's halter.

She opened the stall door and hurried away to the tack room, and he led Frijoles from the stall and into the passageway in the stables.

Teresa returned in no time with a saddle blanket and saddle. She laid the saddle on a nearby bench and placed the blanket high up on the horse's withers. "Let me get the saddle for you," he said.

He handed her the halter and walked over for the saddle, but Richard was already there, lifting it and placing it on the stallion. Once the saddle was firmly cinched, they walked out to the track area, where Teresa saddled up and urged Frijoles into a slow walk.

"They look good," he said, and Richard smiled, but it was a tight, almost brittle smile.

"They do. How are things with the investigation?" the trainer asked and laid his arms across his chest.

Something about the man was suddenly rubbing him wrong. "Moving along. You worried?"

Richard jerked his head toward Matt in surprise. "Me?" he said and tapped a finger on his chest.

Matt nodded slowly. "You. Is there anything you need to tell us?"

Richard blew out a harsh breath and shook his head. "Cops. Always nosing around."

"I'm not a cop. At least not anymore," Matt clarified and narrowed his gaze to examine Richard's face, worried he had misread the man.

Richard looked away and shook his head. When he finally met Matt's gaze again the sadness was evident.

"I had issues. Before Teresa signed me on, I was drinking. Heavily. Lots of rumors about me making mistakes with the horses," the other man said, unshed tears sheening his eyes.

"She trusted you," Matt said, knowing that Teresa's kind heart would have been willing to give Richard a second chance.

"She did, which is why I'd do anything to keep her safe. Get it," Richard said and poked his index finger into Matt's chest. At once, Butter shot to her feet and growled at the man protectively.

"Easy, Butter." Matt signaled the dog to sit with a hand gesture.

Butter whined and held her ground, teeth bared at Richard. "Sit, girl. Sit," Matt commanded, and the dog finally listened.

"I get it and I'll do the same," Matt confirmed with a determined dip of his head.

"Good. If you don't mind—"

"You want to watch the workout," Matt said, and the trainer turned his attention to Teresa as she kicked Frijoles into a slow trot around the track, completing the oval.

As she neared their spot by the rail, Richard gave her a signal and Teresa moved Frijoles into a measured canter, taking him around a few times before pulling up next to them at the rail.

"He feels strong," she said and bent to rub her hand down the horse's shoulders to his chest.

Richard took hold of the reins and stroked the side of the stallion's face. "He does, but let's not push it today. I'll cool him down since I imagine you have things to do," he said and risked a quick look in Matt's direction.

"We do. *Gracias*," she said. She slipped from the horse's back and handed the reins to Richard.

Richard walked Frijoles back to the stables and Matt watched him go, wondering how to raise the issue of the older man's past with Teresa.

"I saw the two of you talking," Teresa said as she took off her riding helmet and let it dangle from her fingertips.

"We were. Richard said you gave him a second chance," he said while they strolled toward the house.

"I did and I wasn't wrong to do it. Richard has been sober for years and has really made a difference around here," she said without hesitation.

"Good to hear." Matt studied her face intently. She had a smudge of dirt on her cheek, and he wiped it away with a finger.

She smiled at the gesture. "*Gracias.* I can get dirty, which is why I'm going to take a quick shower before we head out."

"While you do, I'm going to patrol just to be on the safe side," he said. He had no doubt Sophie and Robbie would have alerted him if they were worried about anything, but he wanted to have his eyes on the property.

She brushed a quick kiss on his lips and rushed away to the house while he headed to the ATV, loaded Butter into the passenger seat and took off to inspect the property.

He wheeled the ATV onto the dirt track that ran between the paddocks, where a number of horses were peacefully grazing. Swinging around to detour around the track, he found everything was quiet as Richard walked Frijoles around the area and then turned him in the direction of the stables.

At the end of the track, he whipped around to run the ATV along the perimeter. But as it had been for the last few days, there was no sign of any activity. A good thing? he wondered. Or were Esquivel and Walker planning something big? Could they even know that the date for the racing commission interview had been moved up?

Because of that, he slowed the ATV for a more thorough examination of the area. Once he reached the front of the house, he detoured to take Butter for a walk around the neighbor's property. There was no new evidence that anyone had been there, maybe because Walker had realized that they'd caught on to his hideout.

Satisfied that nothing was happening at that adjacent property, he loaded Butter back into the ATV and returned to Teresa's home. He walked the shepherd all around the area to make sure everything was secure. He also instructed

Butter to find a scent just in case Walker had been in and around the house, but the shepherd didn't get a hit.

A mixture of relief and worry swept through him as it had before, because sometimes the quiet times could be the most dangerous.

He checked the sliders by the back porch. Locked. Walked back to the front door. Also locked.

Good job, Teresa, he thought, and pulled out the key to let himself and Butter inside.

Teresa was just bounding down the stairs, freshly showered and dressed casually in a teal cap-sleeved shirt that hung freely over faded, curve-hugging jeans. Her hair was loose, the shoulder-length strands swinging around her heart-shaped face and stunning eyes. The color of the shirt brought out flecks of a lighter blue-green in those emerald depths.

"You look…amazing," he said and drank in the sight of her.

A faint splash of pink colored her cheeks and a coy smile swept across her lips. *"Gracias."*

He gestured toward the front door. "Ready to go?"

"Ready as I'll ever be," she said, rushing toward the door and out to her car.

At the car, she held the keys up in the air and jingled them almost in his face. "You should probably drive and keep an eye out for more airboats."

He understood why she was making light of the incident. It made it easier to handle the fact that someone was trying to silence her. He swiped the keys from her hand and said, "I sent you the casino sound Sophie and Robbie isolated. I was hoping it would ring a bell with you. No pun intended."

"Not intended, but still a good pun," she said and hopped into her SUV.

He harnessed Butter into the back seat and climbed into her car.

Teresa was fiddling with her phone as he whipped down the driveway. At the entrance, he waved at the guard positioned there and pulled onto the road for the drive to her parents' casino.

Barely a minute later, the sound of a fake spin was followed by a few electronic tones, another louder whir and then coins dropping into a bucket.

"Totally a slot machine," Teresa said and tapped her phone again to repeat the sound.

He couldn't disagree. "We'll head to the first location we identified with the call detail records and see if there are any slot machines with that same sound."

"What if…what if we can't find it?" Teresa said and nervously shifted the phone back and forth in her hands.

He reached out with one hand and laid it over hers, calming that restless motion. "Let's take this one step at a time."

She forced a smile, but then worried her lower lip with her teeth in a telling gesture. He tightened his hold on her hand, offering a reassuring squeeze while he continued to drive.

Shaking off his hand, she tapped her phone to play the casino sound again and again, as if trying to memorize it. He didn't interfere, using her actions to also store the sound in his mind in the hopes they could identify where Esquivel had been when he'd made the call. Hoping that if they could, maybe someone at the casino would remember seeing Teresa's old trainer and help them track him down.

Thirty minutes later, he pulled into the parking lot at her parents' casino, avoiding Teresa's reserved spot again in favor of one close to the exit so they could easily walk across to the locations pinpointed by the SBS cell phone data analysis. While they walked across together, Butter close to his side, he kept vigilant for anything out of the ordinary.

Nothing. Again. He blew out a relieved sigh and hoped it wouldn't be short-lived.

TERESA GLANCED AT Matt from the corner of her eye. "Ev-erything okay?"

He wrapped an arm around her shoulders and drew her closer. "Everything is okay. Just trying make sure you'll be safe here."

Teresa nodded and they crossed the street and pushed through the door of the small arcade that housed a number of slot machines and electronic gambling games.

Ambling through the space, Teresa focused on the noises bursting from the various machines. Besides the fake spin-ning sounds, a variety of musical tones and beeps signaled wins, but after at least half an hour of strolling around and stopping at a few machines, they hadn't gotten a solid hit.

"Time to head next door," Matt said, and with a nod, Teresa followed him to a slightly larger gaming arcade be-side a small hotel that seemed to catch Matt's eye since he stopped to look at it.

"What is it?" she asked.

Matt dipped his chin in the direction of the hotel. "We don't have any hits from there, but…it's the kind of place you'd use for a 'quick stay,'" he said, emphasizing his words with air quotes.

"Do you think we should check it out?" she asked, and he nodded.

"Maybe later. Let's take a look around this place first since we got a hit here." He gestured with his hand toward the gaming arcade.

As they entered the building, Teresa wrinkled her nose from the stale smell of old cigarette smoke that lingered in the space. Much like at the earlier location, there was an assortment of electronic gambling machines spewing out a cacophony of noises into the air.

They circled around, listening carefully, working the perimeter first. As they neared a side exit door into a common space between the arcade and the hotel, a sound caught her attention.

She laid a hand on Matt's arm to slow him and Butter. "I think I heard something."

Closing her eyes, she focused on the sound, and it came again from the left. She opened her eyes and pointed in the direction of a row of slot machines. "I think it's coming from there," she said and took off toward those slots.

An older man sat on a stool before one, pushing buttons to make the bet. With another push, lights flashed and the reels in the machine went around and around. Lemons, bars, cherries and assorted fruits spun until they came to an abrupt halt. The man did an excited little jump as the machine started playing music and the electronic sound of coins falling resonated in the space.

"That's it. That's the sound," Teresa said excitedly.

The gambler turned to face them, clapped his hands and with a broad smile said, "That's the sound of money, honey."

"It sure is. Do you mind if we watch while you gamble some more?" she asked, well aware from visits to her parents' casinos how superstitious gamblers could be.

"You're my lucky charm. Stay as long as you like," he said. After a few more spins, the sound came again, announcing that he'd won.

This time Matt had his phone ready and recorded the

sound. When he was done, he said, "I'm going to send this to Sophie and Robbie to confirm it's the same sound."

While Teresa understood, she had no doubt this was the same sound from the background of Esquivel's call. Looking around the space, she said, "He was here when he called. And this machine is right near the side exit to the hotel."

"Which means he could have been making a quick escape to that hotel," Matt said and started walking toward the exit, but as he neared it, Butter pawed the ground in a motion that was now familiar to Teresa.

Butter had found Walker's scent.

Chapter Sixteen

"This is so not good. Stay close," Matt said, sweeping his arm around to tuck Teresa behind him.

"Find it, Butter," he said and let the leash have some slack for the shepherd to nose around and stay on the scent.

Head down, sniffing, Butter tracked the smell through the small courtyard separating the two buildings. Near the entrance to the hotel, Butter detoured to a side stairway. After pausing there for a few seconds, she bounded up the stairs, Matt and Teresa almost running to keep pace with her. Two flights later, the dog went up half a flight, but then doubled back, nearly knocking over Matt and Teresa in her haste to return to the floor below.

They rounded the corner and Butter started barking, nearly ripping the leash from Matt's hands.

Matt looked down the balcony connecting the rooms and caught sight of a man moving quickly away from the open doorway of one of the rooms. He wore a Dolphins ball cap and had his head tucked down into the collar of a dark blue windbreaker. His hands were also jammed into the pockets. As Butter continued barking, the man shot a quick look in their direction.

It was Walker.

"Stay here," Matt said to Teresa and raced after the man,

giving chase along the balconies. Butter kept pace with him, straining at the leash and barking.

At the end of the one balcony, Walker flew down the stairs, taking the steps two or three at a time until he reached the ground floor and turned the corner of the staircase.

Matt did the same, Butter jumping down the steps with him, but he lost sight of Walker after he made the turn. But Butter still had his scent and tracked him across the street and into a nearby supermarket.

"Mister, no dogs. Only service dogs," said a burly security guard and blocked Matt's way as he entered.

Matt pulled out an ID. "I'm with SBS. We're tracking a suspect."

The man flashed a quick look at the ID and stepped aside, hands raised in apology. "Sorry, dude."

"Find it," Matt said, and Butter was immediately on the scent again, rushing down the produce aisle and toward the back of the store. At the end of the row, someone had overturned a cart with produce and a clerk kneeled nearby, trying to clean up the mess.

Butter hurtled over the mess and Matt followed. No sign of Walker anywhere but Butter, still in pursuit of him, almost dragged Matt to the far end of the store.

When they reached a door marked Employees Only, Butter pulled away and began pacing back and forth nervously.

"Sit, Butter," he commanded. As he neared the door, he realized why Butter had hesitated. Someone had spilled bleach all along the entrance to the area.

He shoved the door open, and the smell was even stronger in the short hallway. A wet trail of bleach shimmered beneath the overhead lights down the length of the hall.

It was a risk to let Butter walk in the bleach and possibly burn her paws and he worried she'd be unable to pick up the scent again after the smell of the chemicals.

Muttering a curse, he walked back to his shepherd, bent and rubbed her ears, breathing heavily from the run. "You did good, girl. You did good."

Rising, he walked back toward the front door, intending to ask the guard for any security tapes, but as he reached the man, Matt's cell phone started ringing.

Teresa. He answered immediately.

"You've got to get back here, Matt. It's Esquivel. He's been stabbed."

TERESA HUGGED HER arms around herself as the EMTs raised the gurney and rolled it out of the hotel room. The police officer beside her—an Officer Lazlo—said, "Can you tell us again why you were here, Ms. Rodriguez?"

She told herself not to worry that he was looking at her like a suspect, and again repeated what she had told them earlier. "As I said, SBS Agent Matt Perez and I were trying to find Esquivel's location. Agent Perez's K-9 partner picked up a scent—"

"For Esquivel?" the officer said, pen poised over his notebook.

Teresa shook her head vehemently, sending strands of hair shifting against her face. "No, for Finn Walker. SBS and the police think he's responsible for a number of attacks against me and my stables. When Agent Perez and I got to this floor, Walker was running away from this room."

The officer looked away from her and down the hall, drawing her attention in that direction.

Matt was hurrying back with Butter.

"I assume this is Agent Perez and his K-9," Officer Lazlo said with a sharp arch of a brow.

"It is," she said just as Matt joined them.

"SBS Agent Matt Perez." Matt held out his hand to the officer.

The officer shifted pen and pad to one hand and shook Matt's before resuming his questioning. "This young lady…" The officer paused to glance at his pad for the information. "Teresa Rodriguez. Any relation to the casino—"

"Yes, they're my parents but that has nothing to do with this," she said, wishing that the subject of her family and their business wouldn't come up as often as it did.

The officer held his hands up as if in apology and continued, "She says you were here investigating?"

"We were. Our suspect is Finn Walker and we saw him leaving this room a short time ago. I gave chase, but he got away."

"Can you positively identify him?" the officer asked.

"I can. I've also asked the security guard at the supermarket to provide us with the video feeds from their security cameras. They should show Walker running into and out of the supermarket," Matt explained.

"We'll ask for a copy of that security footage as well. Wouldn't want any chain of evidence issues. Officer Perez, wasn't it?" Officer Lazlo said and narrowed his gaze as he examined Matt's face.

"Formerly Officer Perez with the K-9 division. You can also call Trey Gonzalez at SBS for any additional information you may need," Matt said.

At the mention of Trey, the officer's eyes widened. "Detective Gonzalez from Miami Beach PD?"

Matt dipped his head to confirm it. "Retired from the PD now, but one and the same."

The officer closed his pad and tucked the pen into his breast pocket. "I will reach out, Agent Perez. In the meantime, my partner went with the victim to try to get more information from him in case…"

Teresa didn't need him to finish to understand. *In case Esquivel didn't make it.*

"We should get to the hospital as well to find out what we can," Matt said and laid a possessive arm at the small of her back.

Bending his head close, he said, "Are you ready to go?"

She nodded and as they walked away, Matt said, "What happened?"

Teresa sucked in a breath, fighting back the fear that hit her again as she remembered the scene she had walked into just a short time earlier.

Sensing her upset, he stroked a comforting hand up and down her back, giving her the strength to speak.

"When I got to the door of the hotel room, I heard a groan. The door was ajar, and I pushed it open. Esquivel was lying there in a pool of blood. I ran to the bathroom to get some towels and applied pressure to the wounds while I called 911."

"Was Esquivel conscious? Did he say anything?" Matt asked as they crossed the street and returned to her SUV.

"He said Walker's name and that he was sorry. Not much else." She shivered as the memories assailed her. "There was so much blood, Matt. So much."

Matt slipped his hand to her waist, grasped it and turned her into his embrace. "I'm sorry you had to see that."

Battling back tears, she said, "What if he dies? No one deserves that, not even Esquivel."

"Let's pray that he doesn't and can answer some questions for us, including why Walker is willing to kill to keep him silent."

A ROUGH SHUDDER wracked Teresa's body at his words, making him sorry he'd uttered them and reminded her that Walker was out to kill her as well.

"I'm sorry, Teresa. That was thoughtless," he said and continued to hold her until the tension fled her body and she stepped back, wiping away the trails of tears from her face.

"I'm okay. I can handle this," she said and nodded decidedly, as if trying to convince herself of that.

"You already did. If you hadn't acted as fast as you did, Esquivel would have probably died in that hotel room." He walked her over to the passenger side of her SUV.

She hopped up into the SUV and he hurried around to the driver's side, loaded in Butter, got in and quickly maneuvered out of the spot and out of the parking garage.

A tense silence filled the vehicle. As Matt peered at Teresa, he noticed that she was rubbing her hands across her thighs and rocking back and forth slightly in her seat. He reached out and slipped his hand over hers. Twined his fingers with hers and offered her a tender smile.

She smiled back, but it was strained, and tightened her fingers on his. "I'm okay."

"You are," he said, certainty in his tone as he deftly drove one-handed through the streets of Miami and to the medical center where Esquivel had been taken. It took a few spins around the parking lot before he found an empty spot, and barely minutes later, they were in the emergency room.

Together they strode to the desk and Matt pulled out his SBS ID. "Here to see Warner Esquivel. He was just brought in by Miami PD."

The nurse pursed her lips and eyed him but must have decided he wouldn't go away without an answer. She faced her computer, tapped a few keys and then ran her finger across the monitor.

"They've stabilized him, and he should be on his way to surgery shortly. You can wait here. If you need any additional information…" She paused and pointed in the direction of the Miami PD officer who had exited the ER exam room. "You can ask her and unless that's a service dog—"

"It's my K-9 partner," he said and pivoted in the direction of the officer who walked their way as she noticed them by the desk.

"Agent Perez," she said with a respectful dip of her head.

Matt smiled and copied her gesture, offering a friendly nod in greeting. "Officer Vega. Ms. Rodriguez and I are here for Mr. Esquivel."

Vega looked from him to Teresa. "Multiple stab wounds to the abdomen area including a knife wound to his liver and gall bladder. They've taken him to surgery to repair the damage."

Matt handed her his business card. "Teresa and I are going to wait here and would appreciate you keeping us apprised of any developments."

"There's no need for you to be here," the officer said, and her gaze skittered from him to Teresa once again.

"I'd feel better if…I were here in case he… I need to know he's going to be fine," Teresa said, her words broken and stilted.

He laid a hand on her back. "Esquivel used to work for Teresa," he explained.

The officer's eyes narrowed, keenly assessing Teresa. Seemingly satisfied with his explanation, she tapped his card against her notepad and said, "I'll need to check with my superiors about giving you updates."

"I understand, Officer Vega. Any information would be of assistance," he said, and the young officer walked away.

But as she headed to the entrance to the ER where the

police car with her partner had just pulled up, Trey marched through the door and joined them in the waiting room.

Trey stroked a hand down Teresa's arm. "Are you okay?"

AM I OKAY? she wondered and looked away toward the exam rooms. With a shrug, she said, "As well as can be expected."

Trey offered her a sympathetic smile and skimmed his hand down her arm again. "Esquivel owes you his life. Hopefully once he's conscious he'll realize that and help us with this investigation."

She tilted her chin up a determined inch. "And if he doesn't survive?"

"Let's hope that's not the outcome," Trey said.

Matt blew out a disgusted sigh. "Not much of a plan."

Trey nailed him with his gaze. "You're right. It's not. But I've got Sophie and Robbie working on the security feeds from the supermarket. Hopefully they will help identify Walker and once we get the DNA results later, it'll be enough for the district attorney to get a judge to issue an arrest warrant."

Trey gripped Matt's shoulder and squeezed as if to reassure him. "This has been a rough few days. Why don't you take the rest of the day off and go get some rest."

Matt glanced at her from the corner of his eye, and she shook her head.

"We'll just stay a little longer if you don't mind," Matt said, understanding that Teresa needed to be here more than she needed rest.

With a toss of his hands, Trey said, "I guess we wait."

"No need for you to stay," Matt said, but Trey was insistent.

"I want to talk to Esquivel as much as you and the police do. Let's head to the surgical waiting room," Trey suggested, and they walked out of the ER and made their way to the waiting area.

Trey plopped into one of the cushioned chairs and the fake plastic leather groaned with his weight.

Matt slipped an arm around her waist and guided her to a small sofa next to Trey's chair.

She gingerly eased onto the sofa. Matt took the spot beside her and laid his arm across her shoulders.

The movement didn't go unnoticed by Trey, but he said nothing. She was grateful for that. What she was unexpectedly feeling for Matt was all caught up in the maelstrom of emotions surrounding the attacks and what had happened barely an hour earlier.

In her mind's eye she could still picture Esquivel lying there in a pool of blood. Him begging her as he'd seen her and realized the woman he was trying to kill might be his only salvation.

For a hot second she had been tempted to do nothing. To just let him die in the hope that the threat would die with him. But she couldn't and not just because she wanted to know why Esquivel wanted her dead.

She just couldn't let another human being die.

Matt must have sensed her upset since he rubbed her shoulder and drew her closer. "You've got to stop thinking about it."

Maybe in his world that was how you learned to deal with things. You acted when needed and then you stopped thinking about it. But as she met Matt's caring blue gaze, it was clear he was thinking about it. About her and all that had happened.

She offered him a tender smile and cupped his jaw. *"Gracias."*

His brow furrowed and his gaze narrowed in puzzlement. "For what?"

"For understanding. For having my back."

"Always. I'll always have your back," Matt said. Relief swamped her and when he pulled her closer, she nestled into his side.

Trey eyeballed the gesture once again and his lips thinned with worry. Because she didn't want to cause any problems for Matt at work, she straightened slightly and created a little space from him.

MATT GAZED AT Teresa as she put some distance between them. Puzzled, he looked upward, and realizing Trey's interest, he moved his arm away, clasped his hands and hung them between his legs. Needing to dispel the nervous energy in his system, he bounced his legs up and down, mentally counting down the long minutes until a doctor walked out of the staff area.

The doctor wore pale blue scrubs and appeared to be in his early thirties, with short-cropped, black hair. Handsome if those preppy-looking types were your thing.

They rose and the doctor approached, his hazel-eyed gaze guarded beneath a furrowed brow. "I'm Dr. Halston. I'm the surgeon who operated on Mr. Esquivel. Are you here for him?"

"We are. South Beach Security Agents Gonzalez and Perez," Matt said and then gestured to Teresa. "Ms. Rodriguez was a former employer."

The doctor's eyebrows flew upward. "No family?"

Matt glanced at Trey, who said, "Police are trying to track down his daughter. For now, we're here since Mr. Esquivel is involved in a case we're investigating. How is he?"

The doctor hesitated, clearly worried about the breach

in normal protocols, but then, with a slow tilt of his head he said, "Mr. Esquivel came through the surgery but there was substantial damage to several internal organs. He's unconscious right now and should survive, although his recovery will be slow."

Matt nodded. "When can we speak to him?"

A weary shrug lifted the doctor's shoulders before he said, "He may be unconscious for hours, but unless you're family, hospital policy won't permit you to visit."

Frustrated, Matt ran a hand through his hair and said, "Esquivel is involved in several attacks against Ms. Rodriguez. We need to speak to him about those attacks."

The doctor tossed his hands up in the air. "And I need to follow hospital policy. I've already told you too much as it is. If you need anything else, contact the hospital administrator or better yet, have Miami PD interview Mr. Esquivel."

"We had planned to do just that. In the interim, you should know that the man who stabbed Mr. Esquivel is armed and dangerous and may try to finish the job. You should arrange for extra protection for your patient," Trey said and jerked his head in the direction of the elevators.

Matt took the hint and laid his hand against Teresa's back to urge her there, and Trey followed them. At the elevator, Trey pushed the button and said, "We'll ask the PD to work with us to interview Esquivel and put a uniform at his door but that may take some time."

As they boarded the elevator, Trey's phone rang, and he answered. He listened quietly, a grim look on his face that slowly relaxed as his lips tipped up in a smile. "That's good news, Roni. I'll let them know."

He ended the call and faced them. "The PD's DNA results are in and confirm Walker was the one who shot at you. Sophie and Robbie have been able to do screen grabs from the video that show a man who looks like Walker in the supermarket."

"That should be enough to secure an arrest warrant," Matt said as the elevator stopped, and they walked out into the hospital lobby.

"Combined with your testimony it should be. The detectives on the case have finished processing the scene and have asked that you meet them at headquarters so they can interview you," Trey said.

Against his hand, Teresa's body was shaking badly despite the brave face she had put on so far. It hurt his heart to know she was hurting so badly and that he could do so little right now to make her feel better. So he did the only thing he could think to do.

Chapter Seventeen

"I think it's time Teresa went home and got some rest," Matt said, ignoring his boss's request.

Teresa's body trembled with fatigue and nervousness despite Trey's good news about the DNA and video evidence. With a bob of her head, she said, "No, that's okay. I'll go. Anything that will help end this nightmare."

"Detectives Mattson and Cross will be waiting for you. I think you know them, Matt," Trey said with a sharp look in Matt's direction.

"I do. They're good guys, Teresa." He took hold of her hand and twined his fingers with hers.

"I guess we should go," she said, and after bidding goodbye to Trey, they walked out to their car and made the half-hour drive along Miami streets to police headquarters.

Matt parked and they hurried across the brick-and-cement paths in the plaza in front of the building, a low-rise modern structure with dark red columns and mirrored tile. A multistory, rounded tower with more mirrored tile sat like a guard to the left of the entrance with its floor-to-ceiling glass. They pushed through the entrance and to the receptionist desk where Matt asked for the two detectives.

"I'll let them know you're here. Have a seat," the receptionist said but Teresa was too anxious to sit. Instead, they walked to one side of the waiting area and stood by the windows.

"Relax," Matt said as she wrapped her arms around herself and looked away from the waiting room filled with people and out to the plaza area. A white police car emblazoned with green and gold stripes and the police department emblem in gold pulled up in front of the building and parked. Two uniformed officers exited the car, and she recognized them as the officers who had interviewed them earlier.

It was Officer Vega who saw them standing by the windows and walked over as soon as she entered the headquarters.

"I assume you're here to see the detectives?" she asked and when Teresa nodded, she added, "We're headed there as well and can take you."

She and Matt followed the officers, clearing security and riding up to the floor where two detectives were waiting for them. The first detective, an older gentleman, introduced himself. "Detective Dante Mattson. This is my partner, Detective Alicia Cross." He gestured to the younger blonde woman next to him.

"Good to see you again, Perez. Private life seems to agree with you," Detective Cross said with a too friendly smile.

Jealously flared through Teresa and she thrust her hand out. "Nice to meet you. Teresa Rodriguez."

Cross's upturned smile dimmed a bit, and she shook Teresa's hand, not that she had much choice since she'd almost stuck it in the detective's face.

"If you don't mind, we'd like to get your statements on today's incident," Mattson said, a kindly look on the warm brown skin of his face. He motioned them toward a nearby interview room with a sweep of his arm.

Teresa hurried to that room, Matt and the two detectives

close behind her. When she sat, Matt took a spot beside her while the detectives positioned themselves across the way.

She told herself it wasn't "us" against "them" since there was no doubt that she and Matt had nothing to do with Esquivel's stabbing, but somehow it felt that way to her. As Matt twined his fingers with hers and tenderly squeezed, it was almost as if he was reading her mind and trying to quiet her unease.

Detective Mattson spoke first, his voice deep and soothing as if he, too, sensed her anxiety. "We understand there have been a series of incidents directed at you and your business."

"It's why I reached out to SBS," she admitted and glanced at Matt from the corner of her eye.

"And you believe Mr. Esquivel is behind these attacks?" Cross said, her probing gaze drifting between her and Matt.

"Mr. Esquivel and a Finn Walker. I believe you have DNA evidence and a partial print that connects him to the case," Matt clarified.

Mattson and Cross shared a quick, almost disbelieving, look before Cross said, "And this Walker is the individual you saw leaving Esquivel's hotel room?"

Teresa quickly nodded. "Butter—Matt's dog—picked up Walker's scent in the courtyard between the casino and the hotel. We followed Butter and as we reached the second floor, we saw a man walking out of the room. It looked like Walker."

Matt jumped in with, "Butter signaled he was the source of the scent. Butter and I gave chase."

An uneasy silence followed, and Mattson skewered her with his gaze before flipping through his notepad. When he stopped on a page, he paused as if to read it and then said, "When Mr. Perez was chasing the unsub—"

"Unsub?" Teresa asked, not understanding the term.

Matt gently squeezed her hand and said, "Unknown subject, only we know who he is." Matt glared at Mattson and said, "It's Finn Walker. I'm certain you'll be able to pull fingerprints and DNA from whatever was used to stab Esquivel."

"No weapon was found at the location. Where was Esquivel when you entered the room, Ms. Rodriguez?" Mattson said and scrutinized her again, his voice now direct and almost accusing.

Her heart stopped beating for a long second before it started hammering furiously and so loudly she almost didn't hear the detective as he pressed her for an answer. "Ms. Rodriguez?"

"You can't possibly be suggesting that Teresa—"

Cross jumped to her feet and jabbed her finger in the direction of the door. "Mr. Perez. Maybe it's better that you step outside while we speak to Ms. Rodriguez."

Her tone made it clear that it wasn't a suggestion.

Matt slowly rose, but then leaned close and whispered in her ear, "You can do this."

Teresa met his gaze, offered him a strained smile and nodded. "I'll be okay."

With that, Matt left the room and the questioning continued.

"Where was Esquivel when you entered the room?" Mattson repeated.

Teresa splayed her hands on the table, inhaled slowly and then answered. "He was on the floor and there was a lot of blood. I got some towels and tried to do what I could to stop the bleeding. Then I called 911."

Cross leaned forward, closing the distance between

them, and challenged, "You helped Esquivel even though you thought he was behind the attacks against you?"

Teresa held her hands up in a "you're kidding" gesture and parried with, "If you found an…unsub…who was injured, wouldn't you help them even though you thought they'd committed a crime?"

That seemed to set Cross back, since the other woman sank into her chair and said, "Are you willing to provide us with a DNA swab and fingerprints?"

"I have nothing to hide. I did not stab Warner Esquivel," she said with total conviction.

"Great. I'll go get the swab kit and fingerprint scanner." Cross shot to her feet and left the room.

MATT WAS PACING outside the interview room when Detective Cross came storming out and nearly tripped over Butter, who was sitting by the door to the room.

He reached for her arm and stopped her. "You can't possibly think that Teresa had anything to do with Esquivel's stabbing."

Cross glared at his hand, and he shifted away and held his hands up in apology. "Sorry, Alicia."

The apology softened her attitude, but only slightly. "As a former officer, you of all people should know we have to investigate every lead," Cross said.

"Teresa is the victim here. Esquivel is involved in the attacks against her," Matt urged, hands held out in pleading.

"Which gives her a motive to hurt him. She had the opportunity as well since you were off chasing Walker," Cross pointed out and continued, "You might remember that from when you were a cop. We have to investigate every possibility."

She didn't wait for Matt's reply, hurrying down the hall

and leaving Matt to pace back and forth again until she returned with a swab kit and fingerprint scanner. With an angry glare in his direction, Cross swept past him and, avoiding Butter who stood by the door, pushed into the room.

It seemed like hours before Teresa exited the room, pale and shaken, followed by the detectives.

He wrapped an arm around her waist and pulled her close to him. Her body trembled against his and he tried to soothe her. "They just have to investigate every angle."

"I know," she said but her voice lacked conviction.

"Let's head home. Check on Alejandro and his mama," he said and her body visibly relaxed.

"That sounds like heaven." She smiled, only this time the smile reached up into her eyes, turning them a deep green.

"I'm glad it does. Come, Butter," he said, and the dog rushed to Teresa's side as if aware she needed the support.

"Good girl," Teresa said and rubbed the top of her head.

Normally Matt wouldn't want someone petting his K-9 partner, but he suspected Teresa might be a more permanent part of his life in the future. If she was, bonding with Butter would be a good thing.

With that thought, he hurried them out of police headquarters and to Teresa's SUV. As a precaution, he had Butter check the area around the vehicle, but she didn't pick up on any scent. He hadn't thought Walker would be so bold as to come near police headquarters what with all the CCTVs in the area, but he wasn't willing to take any chances.

Once they were in the car and driving to the stables, Teresa said, "Why do you think Walker tried to kill Esquivel?"

That question had been bouncing around in Matt's head since he'd lost Walker in the supermarket and returned to find that Esquivel had been attacked. But all the answers were troubling and would only worry Teresa.

"I really don't know," he said with a reluctant shrug.

Teresa hesitated for a long second. "You do know but you won't say. I can handle it, Matt."

He blew out a harsh breath and shook his head. "I'm sorry. I just don't want to worry you," he admitted.

"Because you think Hollywood sent Walker to tie up loose ends?" she said, voicing his worst fears.

With a nod, he said, "If Hollywood is behind this—"

"It's the worst possible scenario. No one crosses a mobster like Hollywood," she said and inhaled shakily.

"That's true, only... Walker has been careless. Once Mattson and Cross look at all the evidence, there's no doubt Walker is their prime suspect in all of these attacks but that would lead them straight to Hollywood," he mused out loud.

"And Hollywood wouldn't like that kind of attention."

Matt smiled at how quickly she got it. "No, he wouldn't since it might affect his business to have the cops poking around."

"Will the cops poke around?" she asked and peered at him intently.

He did a quick lift of his shoulders. "They should. Maybe once they've exhausted all other leads."

"Which could take a while." She sighed in disapproval.

"Unless we get to it first. I'll call Trey later and see what Roni and he think about talking to Hollywood," Matt said and pulled off the highway to drive the last few miles to the stables.

Brow furrowed, Teresa said, "Do you really think SBS would do that? Do an end run around the police?"

Matt vigorously shook his head. "Not an end run, but the Gonzalez name carries a lot of weight with the PD and Roni is a respected detective. If anyone can get them to move faster, it's the two of them."

TERESA DIDN'T DOUBT the influence of the Gonzalez family. Besides her friendship with Mia, it was one of the reasons she had reached out to them.

"I can't say enough how much I appreciate all that you're doing for me," she said, grateful for SBS and for Matt.

He took hold of her hand. "It's what we do, and as bad as this all is—" he looked away from the road to gaze at her, adoration in his eyes "—I'm glad it's brought us together."

She offered him a shy smile. "I'm glad as well."

He ripped his gaze from her, and they finished the remainder of the drive in silence. As Matt pulled into the driveway, he paused to check with the guard at the front gate. The SBS agent hopped out of his SUV and walked over to the driver's side.

"All good?" Matt asked.

"All's quiet. Nothing unusual. Night-time guard should be here in about an hour to take over," the man said, tapped his hand on the edge of Matt's window and walked back to his SUV to resume his duties.

"Sounds good. Keep us posted," Matt said and drove down to park in front of her house.

He turned in the driver's seat to face her. "It's almost dinnertime, but I assume you want to check in on your horses."

She grinned, feeling much better now that she was home, and he was with her. "I would."

"Let me just text Sophie and Robbie to arrange for them to monitor." He quickly texted and then said, "Let's go."

They hurried to the stables entrance and went straight to Ay Caramba's stall. Joy filled her heart at the sight of the foal nursing from his mother.

"Alejandro looks good," Matt said and sidled up to stand beside her, his hand at her back, stroking tenderly.

"He does. It's such a relief," she admitted. If Alejandro

was as strong a stallion as Frijoles, it would help build her stable's reputation for breeding winners.

"Let's see how Frijoles is doing," she said and they ambled over to the next stall, where Frijoles stood sedately until he noticed them and pranced over to the stall.

"*Hola*, Frijoles. How is *Papi* doing?" she murmured and stroked his face.

The horse snorted and tossed his head, almost as if he were answering. "Yes, you're a good daddy."

"And looking well," Matt said from beside her.

"Looking great. Maybe I'll be able to do a full workout with him tomorrow." She strolled away from him to inspect the rest of the stalls and horses.

Everything was in order until they turned the corner and Luis was suddenly there, pitchfork in hand. He lowered the weapon as he realized who it was.

"*Perdóname*. I heard someone in the stables and wanted to make sure the horses were safe," he said in Spanish.

"*Está bien*, Luis. Everything is okay here," she said, and with a nod, Luis walked back toward the nearby bunkhouse, pitchfork still in hand.

"He's very loyal and responsible," Matt said, and she detected the question in his tone.

"I helped him get a visa so he would be able to stay in the country. We're working on getting him a green card next," she explained. They walked toward the house, stopping halfway to allow Butter to relieve herself.

"That's very caring of you, what you're doing for Luis," he said and paused by the door to the house, searching out her features in the growing dark of dusk.

She gestured to herself. "I know how fortunate my family is to be in America. The kind of freedom we wouldn't have in Cuba. Neither would Luis in his country."

MATT UNDERSTOOD. It was why his grandparents had left Mexico. "I get it, Teresa. My family's story isn't much different."

She smiled, only there was sadness there as she said, "Except I'm sure you've been back to Mexico. It's not the same for Cubans."

"I know that. Trey and I have talked about how hard it is with all the travel issues with both governments."

Teresa blew out a rough breath and unlocked her door. "You can't even imagine. Besides, as hard as it was for my grandparents and parents to leave Cuba, why would they want to go back to a country that isn't free?"

"It wouldn't make sense," he agreed as they walked into the kitchen together. Teresa went to the fridge while he took care of feeding Butter and giving her fresh water.

When he finished, he headed to the counter to stand by Teresa, who had hauled out some hamburger meat from the fridge and was forming it into nice-sized patties.

"Can I help?"

She jerked her head in the direction of the refrigerator. "I've got some potato and macaroni salads in there if you like."

"I like," he said and went to the fridge to take out the salads. He also snagged a string cheese to give as a treat to Butter after the exceptional day she'd put in.

He peeled off the wrapper and fed it to the dog, then placed the salads on the table and then set it.

The smell of beef panbroiling in a skillet soon filled the kitchen, making his stomach growl.

Teresa, spatula in hand, looked over her shoulder at him and smiled. "Hungry?"

Walking over to her, he wrapped an arm around her waist and jostled her playfully. "Starving. I like my burger medium if that's okay. Cheese, please."

"Me, too. Rolls are in that bread box at the end of the counter. I've got sliced cheddar in the fridge."

He dropped a kiss on her temple, grabbed the bag with the rolls from the bread box and got the cheese to hand it to her. He also pulled out mayo, ketchup and mustard and laid them on the table along with the rolls.

Barely a minute later, Teresa came over with the skillet and he scrambled to put the rolls on their plates so she could dish out the burgers.

"Looks delicious. *Gracias*," he said, hugged her and kissed her cheek.

They sat and the meal was silent as hunger drove them to make short work of the burgers and salads.

Matt's stomach was pleasantly full, and he leaned back in his chair to rub it playfully. "That was so good."

Teresa mimicked his actions, grinned and patted her belly. "Very good. How about some coffee and flan for dessert?"

"I won't say no." But as he grabbed his plate and stood, his cell phone chirped.

Sophie calling, which worried him.

As he answered, she said, "A white Jeep is barreling down the drive and it's not ours. Our guard isn't giving chase."

Matt pointed an index finger at Teresa and said, "Please stay here."

"What's wrong?"

Matt signaled to Butter, who immediately came to his side. But Teresa ignored his request and rushed to him.

"What's wrong?" she asked again.

"Trespasser in an SUV. Please listen and stay inside," he said and raced out the door.

Chapter Eighteen

Matt bolted out of the house, Butter loping alongside him, and despite his instructions, Teresa wasn't going to just stand there, especially as a bottle crashed against the corner of the house and a wall of flames erupted across the vinyl siding.

She grabbed a hose, but Matt shouted, "Not water. Get an extinguisher."

A second later he was firing at the Jeep, but the 4x4 did a sharp turn, dipping up onto two wheels for a moment before racing back in the direction of the entrance. As Matt and Butter chased after it, she ran to the kitchen and grabbed a fire extinguisher from beneath the sink. She sprinted outside to tackle the flames licking against the house.

Directing the nozzle at the fire, she squeezed the handle and powder spewed out of the extinguisher. It knocked down the flames closest to the house, but the spray barely lasted a minute. As it ended, she threw the empty canister aside and started kicking up the dirt from the landscaping to tame the last of the fire.

Matt and Luis joined her a minute later and between the three of them they were able to tamp down the last of the flames.

"You okay?" Matt asked and took hold of her hands while Butter sidled up to her side, in protective mode again.

She nodded and rubbed Butter's head. "I am. What happened?"

"I don't know. Let me go check with the guard. Stay, Butter," he said and ran up the driveway to the SUV positioned at the entrance.

Teresa hung back, kicking dirt and stomping the ground where the fire had been to make sure it was well and truly out while Butter sniffed around the edges of the landscaping. Luis nudged loose soil all around the corner of the house where the vinyl siding had melted slightly from the intense flames.

"The fire is out," Luis said and jammed his hands on his hips as he examined the area and bent to check the siding.

"We're good. *Gracias*, Luis," she said and stepped back to examine the damage to the house and landscaping, Butter protectively at her side once again.

Matt came running back. "Guard had just come on duty and got surprised. He was Tasered, probably by Walker."

"Is the guard okay?" she asked and glanced toward the SUV at the gate where a man stood by the vehicle, hand to his head as he shook it as if to clear it.

Matt nodded. "He's okay but shaken. Trey is sending backup guards to secure the property as well as someone to take the guard to the hospital to make sure he's fine."

He stooped down to examine the ground and the house. Standing, he motioned to the remnants of a bottle near the side of the house. "Molotov cocktail. Let me get a bag from the house so I can preserve that evidence."

The sudden shrill sound of sirens blared into the night and a second later, flashing blue and red lights lit the road. A police car turned into the driveway. It slowed by the SUV and the guard stepped over to chat with them and then ges-

tured in the direction of the house. A second later, the police car hurried down and parked in the driveway.

Officers Ventura and Randall stepped from the car and
walked over, a blend of concern and suspicion etched on
their faces. Teresa crossed her arms around herself, worried about both the incident and the earlier questioning
from the detectives.

"Good evening," Officer Ventura said and whipped a pad
and pen from her breast pocket. "We got a call that someone had tried to torch your house?"

Waving his hand in the direction of the entrance to the
property, Matt said, "I'm pretty sure that it was Walker who
Tasered the guard, drove down the driveway and tossed
a Molotov cocktail at the house. I fired at him and gave
chase, but he got away."

Ventura eyed Matt, the damage to the house and then
peered at Teresa pointedly. "Do you have anything to add
to that, Ms. Rodriguez?"

Determined to guard her words and her emotions, she
said, "Nothing else."

The two officers shared a look. Randall returned his attention to her and rocked back on his heels. He was about
to say something when the sound of a car coming down
the drive snared their attention.

A black SUV hurried down while a second vehicle
stopped by the guard at the gate. The black SUV stopped
just behind the police cruiser and a second later, Mia and
Trey hurried out of the car and came to them.

"As soon as Sophie said something was wrong, we
came," Mia said and embraced Teresa.

"Officers. Thank you for getting here so quickly. I'm
sure you understand this has been traumatic for Ms. Rodriguez, so if you don't mind—"

"Detective Gonzalez—" Randall began, but Trey held up a hand in a stop gesture.

"Just a civilian now, Officer Randall. If you don't mind, Ms. Rodriguez has an important meeting tomorrow and needs to get some rest," Trey said and signaled Matt with a jerk of his head.

"Let's go, Teresa," Matt said, wrapped an arm around her waist and led her back into the house, Butter at his side.

After they'd entered and closed the door, she shook her head and pointed at her chest. "I don't get it. They were looking at me like I had done something," she said, tears threatening.

"THEY WERE JUST doing their job," Matt said and slipped his hand down her arm to twine his fingers with hers.

"Then why is Walker still on the loose? Why are they looking at *me* as a suspect?" Teresa lashed out and flung an arm in the direction of the officers outside.

The thud of car doors in the distance made Teresa whirl to face the door and Butter barked at the sound. Barely a heartbeat later, Mia and Trey entered, heads bent together.

"Everything okay?" Matt asked, picking up on their vibes and quieting Butter, who had been nudging his leg, apparently sensing the unease.

Trey nodded. "I've set the officers straight about what's been happening here."

"And the detectives?" Matt asked, ruffling the fur on the dog's head and urging her with a hand gesture to lie down.

"They called me to confirm why SBS was involved, and the discussion went well. I don't think they'll be looking at Teresa any longer." Trey fixed his gaze on her. "Mia and I think it would be best if you went to the SBS penthouse tonight. It'll be more secure, and since the racing commission representative is coming to our offices anyway, you'll be right there."

"What about my horses? The training?" Teresa said, the tone of her voice rising with each syllable.

"We took the liberty of calling your trainer. Richard will come over early in the morning and I'll stay here tonight to make sure nothing else happens," Trey said, jamming his hands in his pockets.

Mia reached out and laid a hand on Teresa's arm. "This makes the most sense, Teresa. You need to keep your head straight for the meeting tomorrow."

Even though Teresa nodded, the tension in her body and tightness of her fingers laced with his warned she was less than thrilled with the possibility. Still, it made sense, so she said, "I just need to pack a few things."

She yanked her hand from Matt's and raced out of the room. Matt was about to give chase, but Trey swept his arm out to stop her.

"Give her a little time to get her head together. Plus, you need to get your things packed. Whatever you need for Butter," he said, then bent and rubbed the dog's head.

"You want me to go with Teresa?" he asked, surprised by the possibility.

"Don't you want to go?" Mia asked, brows wrinkled over her assessing blue-eyed gaze.

Matt tightened his lips and looked away, before shaking his head and blowing out a harsh laugh. "I do. This is more than just a job now. It's personal."

Mia gave a little chuckle and grinned. "I knew it was about more than that before you did, Matt. Why don't you get ready, and I'll drive you, Butter and Teresa back to the SBS building."

He nodded, handed Trey Butter's leash and hurried off.

He tossed his toiletry bag into a duffel he hadn't really unpacked. Down in the kitchen he packed Butter's food and bowls into a reusable shopping bag from a stash that Teresa kept in one of the lower cabinets.

When he returned to the front door, Teresa was already there, clutching an overnight bag with a designer label that said it probably cost more than what he made in a month. Barely days earlier, that would have been a big red stop sign. But now he knew better. Knew her better.

He grabbed hold of Butter's leash from Trey and held out his hand to Teresa. She slipped her hand into his. Her palm was slightly rough, the hand of a woman who wasn't afraid to work hard or get dirty. The hand of the kind of woman who could stand at the side of someone like him.

"Are you ready?" he asked and held his breath as he waited for her answer.

SHE'D LET FEAR dominate her life for the last few days and she was yearning for something different than that tonight. Smiling, she squeezed his hand.

"I'm ready."

"Great," Mia said and clapped her hands. "Let's go before it gets too late. You need to be sharp for your meeting tomorrow."

"I will be," she said, and they bid goodbye to Trey and followed Mia out the door and to the SUV.

"Make yourselves comfortable in the back," Mia said, and they tossed their bags in the trunk area and hopped into the back seat. Butter jumped in, sat between them and laid her head in Teresa's lap. Surprisingly, the dog tried to give an affectionate lick to Teresa's face and she laughed. "Sorry, no doggy kisses."

As Mia drove down the drive, Teresa turned to gaze lovingly at her home, wincing at the sight of the ruined siding. She was nevertheless grateful that they'd been able to put out the fire before any major damage had occurred. But as she'd packed her bag, dozens of questions had bounced around her brain, including why Walker would firebomb her house.

"Do you think Walker knows I'm speaking to the racing commission tomorrow?" she mused out loud while she stroked Butter's head as it lay in her lap, and the dog emitted a satisfied sigh.

Mia met her gaze in the rearview mirror and said, "If he does, he probably got the information from Esquivel."

"Right before Walker stabbed him. But how did Esquivel know? We only just arranged to move up that meeting," Matt said and reached across the width of the seat to hold her hand.

"A leak at the racing commission?" Mia offered.

Teresa tapped the air, connecting the dots between all three. "Which would explain why Walker was trying to scare me off in the first place. Someone tipped off Esquivel and Esquivel warned Walker."

"But if Esquivel and Walker were partners, why would he try to kill him?" Mia asked as she navigated the dark rural roads in Redland.

"To shut him up so he wouldn't talk to the cops?" Teresa said.

Matt shook his head. "Cops don't scare people like Walker, but Hollywood is a whole different kind of scary."

"Are you saying that Walker *and* Hollywood aren't involved in this? That it's just Walker?" Mia said and turned onto Route 1 for the last part of the drive to downtown Miami.

"Hollywood would be pissed either because it could

threaten his business or because they cut him out of the deal," Matt said, still worried that Hollywood had a part in the attacks.

Teresa had worries as well about everything that had happened that day, including why the police would suddenly be looking at her as a suspect. Even though Trey had said that he'd talked to the detectives, it bothered her that they had even considered she could stab Esquivel.

That question and what seemed like dozens of others kept circling around in her brain as she sat in silence, watching the various towns along Route 1 flash by. Comforted by Butter's head in her lap and Matt sitting beside her.

The activity along those smaller towns faded as they reached downtown Miami's business area, quieter now that the skyscrapers were devoid of office workers and rush hour traffic.

In no time Mia was turning into the underground lot for the South Beach Security building and parked in one of the spaces reserved for the Gonzalez family members. She noticed there were a couple of other cars still parked in those spots. *For Sophie and Robbie?* Teresa wondered and didn't realize she'd said it out loud until Mia said, "My cousins are still hard at work. They're trying to see if they could pick up Walker's white Jeep in any of the CCTVs on the main roads."

"There are probably a lot of white Jeeps on the road," she said, sorry that the tech gurus were spending yet another late night on her behalf.

"It's their job and they love solving puzzles like this," Mia said, catching the apology in her voice.

"I appreciate that and everything that you're doing, Mia. I don't know how I could ever repay that," she said as worry of a different kind took hold, namely what the bill from SBS would look like when it came.

Mia swiveled to face her and said, "Like we said when this started, don't worry about that. We take care of our friends."

"Gracias," she said, but as they exited the car and walked toward the elevator, Matt stopped.

"I need to walk Butter before we call it a night," he said.

"We'll meet you in the penthouse. We've coded your badge to give you access to that floor. We'll take your things up," Mia said, making it clear that Teresa should go with her and not Matt.

"I won't be long," he said and walked Butter up the narrow ramp that led to the street.

She watched him disappear out of sight as he turned the corner onto the sidewalk and sighed, missing him already.

"You've got it bad," Mia said and passed a hand down her back to urge her in the direction of the elevator.

She couldn't deny it. *"Sí,* I do and it's a little…scary."

"I get it. I was terrified about what I was feeling for John at first, but Matt is a good man," Mia said and pushed the button for the elevator.

At this time of day, the elevator came down immediately and they boarded to head to the lobby where they cleared security and went to a different set of elevators. Mia tapped her badge against a pad in the elevator and cleared their access to the penthouse.

Teresa had heard rumors about the existence of the exclusive and luxurious space, but nothing could have prepared her for what greeted her as the elevator door opened.

Chapter Nineteen

Matt ambled with Butter along the sidewalk in front of the South Beach Security building. As the shepherd stopped to relieve herself, he gazed at the tall Art Deco–style building that housed SBS. Looking upward at floors with the offices and the penthouse above them, he saw that there were still a number of lights on, because work was a twenty-four-hour responsibility at SBS. But then a light snapped on in the penthouse.

Mia and Teresa.

Beside him Butter barked, as if to remind him to clean up, which he did, and then they hurried into the building. The guards in the lobby nodded as he approached the security desk and he waved and badged himself through the turnstile. Inside the elevator he tapped his badge against the keypad and cleared access to the penthouse.

He'd never been there, since the space was reserved for Gonzalez family members who were working late, important visiting guests or clients who needed extra security.

When the elevator opened on the topmost floor, he walked right into the penthouse apartment and had to stop for a moment to take in the views from the floor-to-ceiling windows that made up the far wall of the open-concept room. Beyond the buildings in downtown Miami, the waters of Biscayne Bay glittered beneath a full moon. To the left, lights sparkled on the MacArthur Causeway and in nearby South Beach. A gleaming white, multistory ocean liner sat in port while beyond that stood the towers on Fisher Island and South Pointe.

The open-concept space of the penthouse was appointed with a mix of modern, lacquer-and-steel furniture and Spanish colonial antiques. A large and comfy-looking leather sectional sat in front of a fireplace and to the right was a high-end kitchen that any top chef would be delighted to use. Just to the side, and close to the floor-to-ceiling windows, was a large glass-and-steel dining table that could easily hold a dozen people. Considering how hardworking the Gonzalez family was, he could imagine that it had been used often by some or all of them during a late night of work.

Matt bent to ruffle the shepherd's fur. "Wow, Butter. This is just…wow."

A sound from beyond the kitchen had them both turning to see Mia and Teresa walking into the kitchen area.

Mia held a key card in her hand and waved it in the direction they had just come from. "The two bedrooms are that way. Teresa's already gotten settled in her room," she said and handed Teresa the key card. "This will give you access to the building, SBS offices and the penthouse."

She walked over to Matt and had to gaze up at his greater height despite the three-inch heels on her Louboutins. "Make yourself at home. Only your two cards will open the penthouse elevator between the hours of 9:00 p.m. and 9:00 a.m. You can buzz us in with this," she said and sashayed to the elevator to point at a button near the doors.

"We'll see you tomorrow. Since the meeting is at two, why don't you come down at twelve for lunch and to get a report on the investigation?" Mia said and hit the button to open the elevator door. She stepped on without waiting for a reply from them, leaving them alone in the silence of the almost cavernous space.

They walked toward each other, stopping in the gap between a coffee table and the fireplace. Staring at each other, uncertain, until Matt took hold of her hand and smiled.

"I'm going to get Butter settled for the night. Why don't you get comfy? Maybe see what's on the television," he said and lightheartedly swung her hand.

As IF SHE could ever get comfortable with the way she was feeling inside, all achy and fluttering from even the simple touch of his hand and the knowledge that they were totally alone in this over-the-top penthouse that rivaled the Presidential Suite in her parents' casino.

"I'm in the bedroom to the right. I loved the views of South Beach." She slipped her hand from his and kissed his cheek.

He smiled again, a tender and understanding tilt of his lips, and strolled toward the kitchen and the bedrooms beyond.

She walked to a wet bar she'd noticed when she'd first come in and poured two fingers of an aged rum into the glasses. Returning to the large sectional, she set out coasters and laid down the glasses as Matt set out Butter's bowls and filled them. He unleashed the shepherd and at his stay command, the dog settled down next to the kitchen island.

Matt sauntered over to the sectional and took a spot next to her. Grabbing a glass, she nestled against him, her back tucked into his side. Her bare feet sank into the butter-soft charcoal gray leather.

Leaning forward, he picked up a glass and wrapped an

arm around her waist, pulling her even tighter against him, her head pillowed on his shoulder.

They sat there for long minutes, sipping their rum, enjoying a peace and quiet they hadn't had in days. The weight of his hand across her midsection was comforting, but it was too easy to imagine him moving it upward to...

She nearly choked on the rum she'd been sipping and set the glass down with a trembling hand. Turning, she kneeled, and splayed her hand across the middle of his chest. His heartbeat pounded strong and erratic beneath her palm.

"Matt... This is... I've never felt this way about anyone." She stroked her hand across his chest and then upward, past the hard line of his collarbone. Pausing by the sensitive skin at the side of his neck, she traced the pulse beating there with her index finger before cupping his jaw and running her thumb across the hard edges of his lips.

They parted beneath her finger as he said, "I never thought a woman like you—"

"A rich girl?" she teased with an arch of a brow.

"You're nothing like any rich girl I've ever known. Like I said before, you're the sun and..." He shook his head and looked away, but she applied gentle pressure to urge him to face her.

Leaning forward until her lips were a butterfly-light brush against his, she said, "I'm just a girl who more than anything wants you to kiss her right now."

DIOS, MATT THOUGHT, but he couldn't resist her any longer because he was just a boy who wanted to kiss her more than he wanted to breathe.

He closed his mouth over hers, savoring the warmth of her lips and the sweet taste of fine rum and Teresa. Kissing her and holding her close until it wasn't enough for either of them.

She shifted to straddle his hips, her center nestled against his hardness. She moaned as she pressed herself to him and kept on kissing him, her hands cradling his face to urge him on.

"Matt, please," she said, and he reached between them and cupped her breast. Her nipple was hard beneath his fingers, and he tweaked it with his fingers.

Her breath exploded against his lips, and she leaned her forehead on his and watched as he caressed her.

The pressure built in his jeans until he knew he couldn't hold off much longer.

"Teresa, tell me now that you want to stop, otherwise—"

"I don't want to stop."

WITH A GROAN that reverberated through her body, Matt surged to his feet with her in his arms, marched through the living room and to the bedroom past the kitchen. He hurried in but stopped dead at the sight of the large king-size bed positioned in the center of the large room across from a wall of floor-to-ceiling windows.

"Mia made sure to tell me all the glass has a privacy film on it," Teresa said and trailed a kiss along the hard length of his jaw.

"Mia never fails to surprise me," he said and rushed to the side of the bed where he let her slip to the floor, her body flush to his. Not an inch of his body wasn't in contact with hers and it was all lean, rock-hard muscle. She ran her hands across the broad slope of his shoulders and down his arms to link her fingers with his.

"She sees things others don't," Teresa said and urged his

hands to her waist as she rubbed her hips back and forth across his hard length.

Matt slipped his hands to her buttocks and stopped the motion but urged her ever tighter to him.

"She does but I don't want to talk about Mia." He eased his hands to her waist to grab hold of her T-shirt and inch his hands beneath to her bare skin. Inch by agonizing inch he slipped his hands up until he was cupping her breasts.

Teresa sucked in a shaky breath and glanced at him as he caressed her, running his thumbs across the hard tips until she moaned and said, "What do you want to talk about?"

A wry grin crept onto his lips, and he chuckled. "I don't want to talk about anything at all," he said and urged her down onto the bed.

His weight pressed her into the mattress for barely a second and then he was standing and jerking off his clothes. His polo shirt flew off, exposing the hard planes of his chest with their smattering of dark brown hair that trailed down his middle to...

She licked her lips as his khakis and briefs hit the floor, exposing him to her. He kicked away the pants and she reached for the hem of her T-shirt, but he stayed her hands.

"Let me," he said, grasped the hem of the shirt and slowly lifted it over her head as she sat on the edge of the bed.

Tenderly he eased the T-shirt over her head, revealing her breasts in her serviceable cotton bra and making her wish she'd worn something sexier.

Maybe next time, she thought as he undid the clasp to bare her breasts to his gaze.

"You're so beautiful," he said and cradled their weight in his hands, teasing the tips with his fingers before kneeling to kiss the tips and then trail a line of kisses down her center until he reached her jeans.

He paused there and glanced at her, asking permission to proceed.

She licked suddenly dry lips and nodded.

He undid the clasp and slowly tugged the denim down until he could snag her panties as well. But as the dark curls at her center became visible, all restraint fled him, and he hurried to yank the jeans off her body.

DIOS, BUT SHE is beautiful. I could kiss her until I don't have breath, Matt thought as he slipped his hands beneath her buttocks to pull her into the center of the bed, where he covered her body with his and kissed her.

He shifted his kisses to her breasts while he slipped his hand down to part her center.

"Matt." She gripped his hand, as if she was afraid of falling.

"It's okay, Teresa. It's okay," he said, and she came apart beneath the first gentle caresses of his fingers.

"I'm sorry. It's been so long," she said as she grasped his wrist to keep him from moving his hand.

He was probably a Neanderthal for being pleased at that confession, but in truth, it had been a long time for him as well.

"Me, too. Give me a second," he said as she released his wrist and stroked her hand up and down along his hard length.

With a low moan, he surged to his feet and left her only long enough to remove protection from his wallet. He tore open the packet and removed the condom, but she took it from his hands and urged him to his back.

Straddling him, she slowly rolled the condom over his length, and he gritted his teeth because her touch nearly undid him.

"Matt?" she asked, hesitating, and he cradled her waist and urged her over him.

"I love you, Teresa."

"*Te quiero*, Matt," she said and sank down onto him, riding him until they were both shaking, breaths rough in between kisses until Teresa's body stilled as another release tore through her.

He murmured soft words of encouragement as her climax ebbed and then he shifted her beneath him, seeking his own release. Driving into her, drawing her ever higher until they both shattered together.

HER HEART GALLOPED in her chest as he lay on his back and nestled her into his side beneath the covers. Under her ear his heart beat a rough rhythm as well and she lazily stroked her hand across his chest until their heartbeats slowed and the first hint of tension crept into his body.

She propped an arm on his chest and leaned her head on her hand to gaze down at him.

"Having second thoughts?"

He pursed his lips and met her gaze directly. "No and… yes. I don't normally mix business with pleasure. I wish we could have met in some other way."

"Only you don't do rich girls," she teased, tugging playfully on his chest hair.

"Only you're not a rich girl, remember?" He mimicked her actions, wrapping a lock of her hair around a finger and pulling on it gently to bring her in for another kiss.

She kissed him and then settled back into his side. "I'm truly not. We were barely breaking even and now with all the costs of the security…"

Her voice trailed off uneasily at the thought of what she would have to pay SBS.

Matt ran a hand down her back and said, "When Mia and Trey said not to worry, they meant it. I don't know how they do it—"

"They're rich," Teresa said, well aware of the Gonzalez family wealth.

With a shrug, he said, "They worked hard for it and don't really shout out about it. Except maybe for Mia, but that's all her money from the social influencing gigs."

"And her husband, John Wilson, I imagine. What's he worth now?" Teresa asked.

"Billions," Matt said in a voice that mimicked Dr. Evil.

She laughed as he intended and soothed a hand across his chest again. "I'll try not to worry about that since there's so much else to worry about," she said as the pleasure from the earlier lovemaking slowly faded and the reality of her situation crept in.

Matt flipped onto his side to face her. Cradling her cheek, he urged her to meet his gaze. "We're almost at the end of the race, Teresa. Tomorrow we'll know why the racing commission wants to talk to you and hopefully that will tell us why Walker and Esquivel don't want that to happen."

More than most, Teresa knew there were no guarantees at the end of any race. The upsets when a dark horse beat the odds. She wanted to think of herself as that dark horse that came out a winner.

I'm already in the winner's circle with Matt, she thought and inched upward to kiss him, wanting to restore the earlier happiness she'd experienced in his arms.

As he pressed her into the mattress and pinned her there with his body, she lost herself in the joy of his loving and the possibility of a future with him.

Chapter Twenty

For the rest of the night and through the morning, Matt did his best in a variety of ways to keep Teresa from thinking about what she would have to do later that day.

They'd made leisurely love while watching the sun come up over Biscayne Bay. After a short nap, they'd made love again while they showered together. Together they'd cooked breakfast and eaten it at the dining room table, tossing bits of bacon to Butter who eagerly ate the treats.

He'd left Teresa only long enough to take Butter for a morning walk.

When he'd come back up to the penthouse, Teresa was standing by the wall of windows, arms wrapped around herself. Back ramrod straight in a gesture he recognized well. She had dressed in a sedate black dress, her hair up in some fancy kind of topknot, probably to look more formal for the interview.

She was preparing herself for what would happen in a couple of hours.

She turned as he walked in and managed a smile, but deep brackets beside her lips warned of her strain. "Richard called. He said the workout went well today. He also said everything was calm at the stables. No more incidents."

He unclipped Butter's leash and the shepherd lay down by the edge of the sectional at his hand command. Walking over to Teresa, he stroked his hand down her arm to twine his fingers with hers. "That's good to hear. It's almost time for lunch. Do you want to head down to the SBS offices?"

She slowly inhaled, held her breath, exhaled and then nodded. "It's as good a time as any."

With a quick dip of his head, he led her to the elevator, stopping only to leash Butter again. They stood shoulder to shoulder in the elevator, Butter sidling up to Teresa, who smiled and patted the dog's head.

As they entered the reception area, the young Latina at the desk smiled and quickly seated them in the conference room just behind the desk. When they sat side by side at the table, the receptionist hit the button to make the windows opaque and give them privacy.

"They've thought of everything," Teresa said as she peered at the now milky white wall.

In the six months that Matt had been working for SBS, he'd realized the same thing. "They're very thorough. It's why their business is growing, like the new K-9 division Trey added." He patted Butter's head as the dog sat beside him in the gap he'd made by moving one of the conference table chairs.

A knock on the door came before Trey walked in, followed by Mia, Sophie and Robbie. "Good afternoon," Trey said and laid a leather portfolio on the conference room table. "We have lunch coming up in about ten minutes. After that we'll call Roni to get an update on the police investigations."

"Sophie and Robbie are also going to share anything new with Roni so she can report back to the detectives working the case," Mia said as she took a spot next to her brother, while Sophie and Robbie sat across from them and next to Matt and her.

"*Gracias.* Your quick thinking saved my house last night," Teresa said, glancing at the tech gurus who had been so helpful.

They smiled, looking so much alike it was as if they were almost twins despite the nearly two-year age difference between Robbie and his younger sister.

"Anything for a family friend," Sophie said and laid a hand on Teresa's to reassure her.

The conference room phone chirped, and Trey answered. "What is it, Julia?"

"The food is here. May we bring it in?" the receptionist said.

"Of course. Come on in," he said and a second later, Julia opened the door and directed the delivery people on where to set up the sandwiches, salads and sodas on the large credenza at one side of the conference room.

Once they'd left, Mia said, "*Por favor,* help yourselves."

Robbie nearly bolted from his chair, leaving Sophie to roll her eyes and chuckle. "He's always hungry."

She rose and walked over at a more sedate pace, as did Mia and Trey.

When Teresa didn't move right away, Matt leaned close to her. "Aren't you hungry?"

IT WASN'T JUST that they'd had a healthy breakfast earlier that morning. A weird combination of knots and butterflies alternated in her stomach, almost painful in intensity.

Teresa ran a hand across her midsection and said, "More like nerves. I'm not sure I can keep anything down."

He nodded, understanding. "I'll get you something and maybe you'll feel more like eating after we hear what Roni, Sophie and Robbie have to say."

She wasn't sure she would feel like eating but didn't

argue with him as he rose and returned a few minutes later with two plates piled with food. He left her again to retrieve two sodas and placed one in front of her. Thanking him as he set the plate in front of her, she sat there in silence for several minutes, sipping her soda, while others satisfied their hunger before Trey made the call to Roni.

Trey peered around the room and focused on her still uneaten meal. "Are we good to call Roni? Teresa, are you okay?"

She nodded, and to ease Trey's worry, she poked at the potato salad on the plate before forking some up to eat.

Seemingly satisfied with that, he dialed Roni, who immediately answered. "*Hola, mi amor.* I have some good news for you," she said.

"That's good to hear," Trey said and glanced her way again.

Teresa ate another forkful, and in all honesty, maybe they'd had the right idea since the food traveled down easily and seemed to be calming the battle raging in her belly.

"Police recovered a bloody knife from under the bed in the hotel room. Walker's prints were all over it. Teresa is no longer a suspect in Esquivel's attempted murder," Roni reported.

Relief swamped her and the fork slipped from her nerveless fingers and clattered on the table.

Matt stroked his hand across her shoulders and leaned close to whisper, "You okay?"

With a shaky breath, she said, "I'm better now."

She picked up the fork and some more salad, as if to prove she was truly okay, and Trey continued with the call.

"Anything else to report?" Trey pressed his wife.

"The DA is asking for an arrest warrant for Walker and—" Roni paused and the muffled sound of her voice speaking with someone else drifted across the speaker before she returned to the conversation.

"We just got word that Esquivel is conscious. Mattson and Cross are on their way to interview him. Hopefully he can provide additional information on Walker and his whereabouts," Roni said.

"Maybe we can help with that. Mia's John gave us access to his software, and we were able to predict possible routes that Walker would use to leave Teresa's place," Sophie said, and Robbie jumped in with, "Using those predicted routes, we picked up Walker's white Jeep in some CCTV footage after his last attack."

"Tell me it's good news," Roni said.

Robbie grinned, his light blue eyes alive with excitement. "We were able to trace the Jeep onto Southwest 248th Street. We worried we'd lose him if he got on the highway, but he just kept on going straight until he turned off. We think he went to Black Point Park."

"There's a marina and restaurant there, right?" Mia asked, forehead wrinkled over her blue gaze.

"There are. We're trying to tap into the CCTVs at the marina and restaurant to see if we can confirm that Walker is in that area," Sophie explained.

"Great work, *primos*. I'll let the detectives know so they can get some uniforms to canvass the park," Roni said, thanking Trey's cousins for their excellent work.

In the background another voice came across the line, prompting Roni to say, "I've got to go. We have a lead on another case."

"Cuidaté, mi amor," Trey said, his gaze warm and full of adoration as he asked her to take care.

Like the kind of adoration in Matt's eyes as he once again stroked her back and glanced at her.

Smiling, and finally feeling as if they were close to the end of her nightmare, she grabbed her sandwich and ate.

MATT WAS GLAD to see that Teresa's anxiety had dimmed enough for her to eat. He worried her calm wouldn't last once the racing commission rep arrived to do his interview or until Walker was in custody.

"I know having the uniforms canvass Black Point makes sense, but I'd rather go with Butter and check it out myself," he said.

Butter sat up at the mention of her name and gave him her attention. He snagged a bit of ham and cheese from the last piece of his sandwich and fed it to the shepherd as a treat.

"I agree and I'd like to go with you as soon as the racing commission rep arrives," Trey said.

Teresa's body jumped beside him, probably at the thought of tackling the interview without him at her side. He hesitated, unsure that leaving Teresa alone for the talk was a good idea.

"Matt?" Trey said and flipped a pen from tip to top over and over on the surface of his portfolio.

Mia reached out a hand to stop her brother's nervous gesture. "If Teresa would prefer not to be alone, I can stay with her."

Matt peered at Teresa. Deep slashes framed the edges of her tight lips and her pupils seemed huge in her emerald gaze.

"I can stay—"

"No, it makes sense for you and Butter to track down Walker," she said and vehemently shook her head, shaking loose strands of hair from her fancy topknot.

Teresa looked at Mia and her smile relaxed the tiniest

bit. "*Gracias*, for volunteering to stay with me. I really appreciate that."

"*Bueno*, so we're set. Let's finish lunch so we can all get to work," Trey said, hopped up from his chair and returned to the credenza to grab another piece of sandwich.

Mia chuckled and leaned closer across the broad width of the conference room table. "He thinks that if Roni is eating for two, he should also," she teased her older brother.

Trey shook his head, laid the plate on the table and flexed his arms. "Not an ounce of flab, *hermanita*," he shot back.

Matt laughed at the siblings' interaction and from the corner of his eye caught Teresa's action as she picked up her own sandwich and ate.

A good thing, he thought and sat back to take in the discussions as Trey and Mia spoke to their tech guru cousins on what their next steps would be. Sophie flipped on a large monitor on the far side of the conference room and pulled up a satellite image of Black Point Park. Using a laser pointer, she highlighted where they'd lost sight of Walker's Jeep on the nearby road and also the location of the restaurant and other buildings in the park.

"My money is on him being in one of those vacant boats," Matt tossed out for consideration, thinking about how Walker had used the absent neighbor's home as a hideout.

"I agree," Trey said, rose and approached the monitor. "There's a walkway that skirts the marina. Walker could use it to access the docks there." He pointed out the path in the satellite view.

"If he's been there, Butter should be able to pick up a scent," Matt said and reached down to pat his shepherd's head.

"Good. So it's agreed that Matt and I will check out Black Point, Sophie and Robbie will continue to try to get eyes on Walker, and Mia and Teresa will deal with the racing commission rep," Trey said, returned to the table and sat.

"It is," Teresa said, although still clearly hesitant.

"It's what makes sense. If Walker is at the marina and Butter can track him down—"

"It'll end this nightmare," she finished for him. Offering him a smile filled with resignation, she said, "I understand, and I'll be fine with Mia at my side."

"You will be, *amiga*," Mia chimed in from across the table.

Not wanting to waste another moment, Matt said, "If we're done with lunch, I'd like to go to Black Point Park."

Trey nodded and pushed to his feet. "I'm with you. If you don't mind, we'll be on our way."

Matt unfolded his length from the seat and, uncaring of how unprofessional it might look, brushed a quick kiss across Teresa's temple. "Don't worry. Walker's days of freedom are numbered."

Chapter Twenty-One

Teresa didn't think she could be quite as sure as Matt about finally apprehending her attacker. But as the Gonzalez cousins exited the room, leaving her alone with Mia, she stared across the table at her friend and said, "How can Matt be so sure? Walker's been one step ahead of us the whole time."

"He has managed to surprise us more than any of us would like, but Sophie and Robbie's lead seems solid. If they're right, Walker has boxed himself into a corner."

"Unless he escapes by sailing away," Teresa said and waved a hand to mimic his gliding free.

"Not this time. I just feel it in here," Mia said and tapped a finger to the middle of her chest.

"I hope you're right," Teresa said but couldn't stop worrying not only about Walker escaping, but about Trey's and Matt's safety.

Ever observant, Mia said, "They'll be fine. They're both licensed to carry, and Butter is a weapon as well when needed."

It was hard to picture the protective shepherd with her goofy tongue and melty chocolate eyes as dangerous, although K-9s were often trained to attack.

Not wanting to continue the conversation, Teresa shot a quick look at her cell phone. "It's almost time."

Mia peered at her pricey, gold-and-diamond Pasha de

Cartier watch, just like the one Teresa had sold to pay some of her stable's expenses. "It is. We'll be meeting in another of our conference rooms. Do you need to take a break before we go there?"

That morning's coffee and lunch were warning her not to delay, especially if the meeting with the racing commission representative went longer than she expected.

"I do need a break. It'll be good to stretch as well," she said, unused to spending so much time sitting or idle. Although she could really get used to spending time with Matt in bed once this was all done.

She met Mia by the door to the conference room and they strolled down the hall together, chatting about the new foal as well as an upcoming party at a local country club to which they'd both been invited. Once they were finished in the women's room, Mia escorted her to a smaller but well-appointed conference room next to the larger one they'd just vacated.

Mia was just pouring her a glass of ice water when the conference room phone chirped. She answered and then said, "Please show them in."

Them? Teresa wondered. She'd expected only one representative from the racing commission.

Two men came to the door of the conference room and Mia invited them to enter.

Teresa recognized one of the men from the New York races in which her horses had run. The man with him screamed "cop" with his black suit, starched white shirt and black-and-red striped tie. Her guess was confirmed as he reached into his jacket pocket and pulled out a badge.

"Ms. Rodriguez. Special Agent Rick Santoro," he said and offered her his hand.

She shook it and glanced at the familiar man. "Mr. Bab-cock, if I remember correctly."

"You did, Teresa. May I call you Teresa?" he said and shook her hand effusively, dimming by the barest amount the anxiety she was feeling from the presence of the FBI agent.

"You may. This is Mia Gonzalez. She and her family run South Beach Security and I've hired them for protec-tion, but I'm sure you're aware of that already," she said as Mia shook both men's hands and then urged everyone to take a seat.

"We are and I'm sorry if our investigation is somehow responsible for placing you in jeopardy," Babcock said. He set his briefcase on the tabletop, opened it and extracted a large file.

"A heads-up about the danger might have been nice, Mr. Babcock," Mia said, her tone so frosty they probably didn't need air conditioning in the room.

"I'm afraid I'm to blame," FBI Agent Santoro said and laid a large hand across the front of his chest.

"Care to explain?" Mia said, clearly ready to fight on Teresa's behalf. Teresa was grateful for that. Mia probably had way more experience with FBI types like Santoro than Teresa ever could.

"First, we'd like to ask Ms. Rodriguez some questions," Santoro said and glanced in Babcock's direction.

Babcock opened the file and nervously flipped through papers, scattering a few on the tabletop before he yanked out a photo and slid it across the table to Teresa.

"Do you know this man?" Babcock asked.

It was a grainy black-and-white photo of Walker with a racehorse. He had the beard and longer hair that had made her not recognize him at first, but she now had no doubt about who he was.

"It's Finn Walker, only he's clean-shaven and has a buzz cut now." She was passing the photo back to Babcock when she noticed something familiar. "This photo's from one of the Saratoga races, right?"

"It is. You're very observant," Babcock confirmed, retrieved the photo and then passed over a list of about ten or so races that had occurred the year before.

Teresa scrutinized the list but was puzzled by it since it contained races in which she hadn't participated. "I don't understand."

"You raced a number of horses last year. Can you identify at which of these races?" Santoro asked.

She was starting to get the feeling she'd had yesterday with the two detectives and was about to speak when Mia stretched her arm in front of Teresa to stop her.

"Unless you can give us some rationale for this line of questioning, Teresa may wish to ask for the presence of a lawyer," she said.

Santoro glared at Mia. "Ms. Rodriguez is not in custody, so there is no need for a lawyer."

The FBI agent was clearly underestimating Mia's tenacity. A pit bull would give up more easily than Mia.

"Nevertheless, we'd like to hear your rationale before continuing."

Santoro gritted his teeth and the muscles in his jaw clenched from the force of it. A too long and very hostile glare focused on them before he said, "Go ahead, Babcock."

Almost timidly, Babcock gestured to the list. "That is a list of races that we suspect were fixed."

"Fixed, as in—"

"Walker paid off the owners or jockeys to change the

results and was aided by Esquivel, who doped the horses if they didn't agree," Santoro clarified.

Teresa held her hands up and waved in a hold on gesture. "And you think I took part in that? I run a clean business and I didn't even have entries in quite a few of these races."

Babcock coughed uncomfortably and looked at the agent again, as if seeking permission. When the agent nodded, he said, "We don't think you have anything to do with the fixes. But we believe you may have seen Walker with the horses in question. Do you think you can identify when you saw him in the stable areas?"

Teresa shared a look with Mia and at her friend's go-ahead lift of her chin, she picked up the list and reviewed it carefully, trying to recall when she might have seen Walker. When she examined it, she realized she had seen him in at least four or five of the races on the list.

Placing the list in the middle of the table so that Babcock could see it, she pointed to the entries. "I think I saw him at these races."

"Are you sure, Ms. Rodriguez?" the FBI agent pressed.

She nodded emphatically. "I'm sure. Is that why Walker wanted to stop me from talking to you?"

"It is. As a witness, we'll need you to testify—"

Mia raised a petite hand in the air to stop him. "Who else is involved in this fixing scheme? Tony Hollywood?"

The red flush creeping up the FBI agent's face warned he wasn't a fan of Mia interfering. Despite that, he reluctantly answered, "We have no evidence that Hollywood was involved, although he is a target of another investigation we're running. Walker appears to have been acting only with Esquivel."

Mia was about to push the agent again until Teresa laid a hand on her friend's arm. It was a surprisingly calm hand, maybe because it was reassuring to know that the danger might end with Walker's apprehension since Hollywood wasn't a part of this scheme.

"We can discuss my testifying once Walker is in custody," she said.

Sensing they were done for the day, Babcock jumped to his feet, hastily stuffed everything back into the briefcase and slammed it closed. "We appreciate that, Teresa. Again, we're so very sorry for all the trouble you've had."

"And I'm sure you'll make it up to me by bearing the costs of all the damages that occurred to my home and business because of your failure to act," Teresa said and rose from her chair.

Babcock stuttered and stumbled, and Santoro jumped in to save him. "I'm sure Mr. Babcock can discuss that with his superiors."

Santoro held out his hand to Mia. "I wish I could say it was a pleasure," he said, but with a hint of humor offsetting the dig.

"The same, Special Agent Santoro," Mia said, shook his hand, and then did the same with Babcock.

Teresa waited and then offered her goodbyes to the two men, but as they were walking out the door she said, "By the way, you may want to check for a leak in your office. After last night's attack, I'm sure Walker knew we were meeting today."

Santoro dipped his head. "We'll take that under advisement," he said, and Mia escorted the two men from the room.

When her friend returned, she sat in the chair, and they faced each other. Mia took Teresa's hands in hers and said, "It's good news that Hollywood isn't part of this."

"It is and let me say, I'm glad I had you in my corner.

How did you learn to handle people like Santoro? He was kind of intimidating."

Mia threw her head back and laughed, an almost musical sound that had Teresa smiling.

"You forget Trey is my older brother. Even before he was a marine or a cop, he'd grill me if I came home even one minute late," Mia said but there was no doubting the love and affection for her overprotective sibling.

"You handled them pretty well yourself," Mia added and chuckled.

Teresa likewise laughed, imagining what it must have been like to have an alpha like Trey as a brother. But with that came the niggle of fear once more at what Trey, Matt and Butter would encounter at the marina.

"Tell me again they're going to be all right," she said.

Mia squeezed her hands and drew her in for a long hug. "They're going to be all right," her friend said, but the slight shiver in her body and waver in her voice indicated she was also worried about the two men.

When they separated, Mia said, "How about we go up to the penthouse and you can tell me more about your new foal while we wait to hear from them?"

Teresa slowly pushed to her feet and held out a hand to her friend. "I think that sounds like heaven."

Chapter Twenty-Two

Matt sat silently beside Trey, who hadn't said much either since they'd left the SBS offices, but Matt was sure Trey was processing the kiss he'd witnessed earlier in the conference room. When his friend tossed a quick glance in his direction, Matt braced himself for the question he was sure would follow.

"You and Teresa. I'm not normally in favor of our agents becoming involved with clients, but…tell me it's not just a fling," Trey said, knuckles white on the wheel from the pressure of his grip.

"It's not a fling. I'm in love with her," Matt admitted.

"Teresa is an amazing woman, but…" Trey's voice trailed off and his worried glance said it all for Matt.

"You don't want me to get burned by another rich girl," Matt said with a laugh and shake of his head. "I get it, Trey, only like you said, Teresa is an amazing woman. She's nothing like the girl who ruined my life."

"No, she's not. Remember that and don't break her heart," Trey warned.

Matt shook his head again and teased, "Or I'll have to deal with you."

A sharp bark of a laugh and wry grin escaped Trey's lips. "*Hell*, no. You'll have to deal with Mia."

Matt held his hands up in surrender. "*Dios mio*, anything but that."

"Good," Trey said and pulled into the parking lot for the restaurant in Black Point Park. He stopped the car, faced Matt and said, "Let's go."

Matt hopped out of the car and opened the back seat to free Butter from her harness and clip on the leash. Rubbing the shepherd's head, he said, "You're a good girl. You're going to find him, aren't you?"

Butter gave a little woof and licked his face. "That's it. A good girl."

He eased the dog from the back seat and walked toward the rear where Trey had popped open the back hatch of the SUV. Trey handed Matt bulletproof vests for both him and Butter.

At Matt's raised eyebrows, Trey slipped on his vest, and said, "No sense taking any chances. Walker is way too dangerous."

He couldn't disagree. Bending, he slipped the vest on Butter and then tugged on his own vest, making sure that he could easily reach the gun tucked into the holster at the small of his back.

Once they were suited up, they hurried to the restaurant perched at the tip of land next to the water. Metal-roofed, hut-like buildings were open to the fresh air and surrounded by tables and brightly colored shades to protect patrons from the sun.

They approached the hostess stand and the young woman's perfectly manicured eyebrows flew up at the sight of them in their SBS-branded vests. "H-h-ow m-may I h-h-elp you?" she stammered.

Trey handed her a photo of Walker. "Have you seen this man around?"

With a shaky hand, she took the photo and peered at it. Shrugging, she said, "Maybe. He's got a scruffy blond beard and wears a beanie a lot."

Matt glanced around the restaurant, which had both open-air and indoor seating, but didn't see anyone matching that description. "Has he been in today?" he asked.

The hostess shook her head and handed the photo back to Trey. "No. Not yet."

"Did you see where he came from?" Trey asked and likewise did a quick sweep of the area to look for Walker.

"No. It can get busy at night. People are coming off their boats and want drinks and a meal," she explained.

"If you see him, be careful and call 911. Ask for Detectives Mattson or Cross or you can call us," Trey said and handed the young woman his business card.

"Got it." She laid the card on the hostess podium with a nervous look at them.

As they sauntered away from the hostess, Trey tracked his gaze all across the park property. "Left or right?"

"Let's let Butter make the choice. Find it, girl," Matt said, and Butter immediately went to work, sniffing around the thick grass along the edges of the path leading from the restaurant and toward the larger set of docks to the left of the dining areas.

Matt and Trey followed the shepherd as she searched for the scent and as they did so, they caught sight of Mattson and Cross speaking to a couple at the end of a dock. It was the farthest one from the restaurant and judging from the headshakes of the couple, they hadn't seen Walker around.

Matt took a long look around the grounds to decide where to go next since the docks searched by the officers seemed to be a bust. Next to the docks was a path that fed into the Black Creek Trail, which ran on both sides of the water. The trail also wrapped around the restaurant toward a smaller set of docks. It worried him that if Walker had access to a boat there, he could easily use Black Creek to escape into Biscayne Bay.

"There's nothing for him in that direction," Matt said, pointed to the path and looked toward the restaurant. "Let's head back that way."

"You're the boss," Trey quipped, but followed Matt's lead as he commanded Butter to find the scent again.

Nose down, the shepherd searched the ground, but didn't hit on anything until they reached the steps for the restaurant's waterside dining area. At the steps, Butter hesitated and sniffed back and forth across the steps. A second later, she pawed the ground and Matt said, "Good girl. Find him, Butter. Find him."

The shepherd took off at a faster pace, head bent low as she followed the scent, weaving in and out through the tables where patrons sat enjoying meals and drinks. People seemed shocked at the sight of them with their vests as they hurried past, led by the dog who had zeroed in on Walker's scent.

They reached the end of the dining area and Butter rushed along a cement path that led back to a circular parking lot. The shepherd nosed around the trees and grass there, and tugging on her leash, cut through the landscaping and to the smaller group of docks. Unlike the other marina area, where dozens of boats were moored, there were only six or so boats secured in this area.

Butter urged them on, straining at the leash, but as they neared the first dock, a man with a beanie emerged from the cabin of a small boat. As he noticed them, he stopped short, whipped out a gun and opened fire.

The first shot caught Matt in the ribs, driving the breath

from his body and freezing him in place from the shock of the blow.

Trey grabbed the back of his vest and hauled him behind the cover of a car parked nearby. Butter quickly came to his side and at his command, stopped straining at her leash and sat beside him.

Matt muttered a curse as the pain of the impact finally registered. Bullets pinged against the metal as Walker kept on firing at the car.

As the shots ended and the empty click of a revolver registered, Matt risked a glance around the edge of the bumper. Walker was undoing the ropes from the cleats on the dock to make his escape in the boat.

"Not going to happen," Matt said and pushed to his feet, gun trained on Walker.

Trey followed him, weapon also drawn, and shouted, "Stop right there, Walker."

But Walker kept trying to undo the ropes and Matt knew there was only one way to stop him in time. He released Butter's leash and gave the attack command. *"Útok."*

Butter galloped down the dock and threw herself at Walker, driving him down onto the wooden planks. She bit his arm to keep him in place while Walker thrashed and kicked, trying to free himself.

As Matt reached them, he trained his pistol on Walker and called off Butter. The dog released Walker and sat at Matt's side, but leaning forward, ready to attack again.

Trey flipped Walker onto his stomach and pinned him down with a knee in the middle of his back. He was reaching for his zip ties when Mattson and Cross came rushing down the path toward the dock, apparently having heard the shots.

"I think you can take it from here," Trey said, but waited for Cross to take out her restraints and secure Walker.

Once the restraints were in place, Trey slipped off Walker and the detective hauled him to his feet. "Finn Walker. You're under arrest for the attempted murder of Warner Esquivel and Teresa Rodriguez," Cross said and then started a recitation of the Miranda rights.

Since the situation was under control, Matt and Trey walked back to their SUV for the return trip to the SBS offices. But as they reached the SUV and Matt slipped off the vest, he groaned at the pain in his side and rubbed the tender area.

"We should have someone take a look at that," Trey said.

Matt shook his head. "Nothing broken. I'll be okay."

"I'll feel better when a doctor tells me that," Trey said, and as eager as Matt was to get back to Teresa and let her know her ordeal was over, he knew better than to argue with his boss and friend.

Teresa had wanted to rush to the ER as soon as they'd finished the call from Trey and Matt, worried that Matt's injury was worse than what they were admitting. But Mia had calmed her down, reassuring her that Trey wouldn't let Matt take any chances and that they should wait for them in the penthouse.

The hour seemed more like twenty-four as she paced back and forth in front of the windows, waiting for Matt's, Butter's and Trey's return.

When the whooshing of the elevator doors announced their arrival, she rushed there and nearly launched herself at Matt as he stepped off.

His rough groan and indrawn breath worried her, but he wrapped his arms around her and held her tight. "I'm okay," he said and Butter gave a little bark from his side, as if to confirm it.

Realizing that her exuberant welcome might have caused pain, she said, "I'm sorry. I didn't mean to hurt you."

With a tender smile, he cradled her jaw and said, "Just bruised. Nothing to worry about."

He wrapped an arm around her waist and walked with her deeper into the penthouse as Trey walked over to Mia and hugged his sister. With a hand command, Butter sat at their feet, patiently waiting.

"It's over. Walker's in custody and Esquivel will survive. DA is already speaking to Esquivel to try to get him to flip on Walker," Trey said and peered in her direction. "Roni will keep us posted on whether Walker makes bail. In the meantime, we'll keep our guards in place at your location."

"I'll go home with you if you want, Teresa," Matt said and tightened his grasp on her waist.

"I want, Matt," she said, prompting Mia to grab her brother's hand and tug him toward the elevator.

"I think it's time we go, *hermanito*," she said and pushed the button to open the elevator door.

"We'll keep you posted," Trey said as they boarded and the door closed, almost in his face.

ONCE THEY WERE ALONE, Matt faced her. "Are you sure you want me to go with you?"

She offered him a lopsided grin and stroked her fingers across his cheek before cupping his jaw. "I want that more than anything, Matt. I want *you* more than anything. I hope you want the same thing."

"I do. I never thought I would say that about someone like you—"

"Because of what happened before?" she said, brow furrowed over those amazing emerald eyes.

He nodded. "Because of that, only there you were sleeping with your horse and then standing there dripping in I don't know what after birthing that foal. And when you ride, it's like seeing the wind."

She did that lopsided grin again and ran a hand through his hair. "I thought I was the sun?" she teased, reminding him of what he'd said days earlier.

He chuckled and shook his head. "You're that, too, Teresa. I love you and I want to spend the rest of my life finding out everything about you."

She rested her forehead on his and locked her jewel-like gaze on him. "And I want the same, Matt. I want to spend the rest of my life learning everything about you."

Matt kissed her and hugged her tight and at their feet, Butter gave a little bark, jerking them apart.

Laughing, Teresa kneeled and rubbed the dog's ears playfully. "And spending time with you, too."

Butter licked her face, earning a wrinkled nose from Teresa as she stood again. "I'm not a big fan of doggy kisses, but I guess I'll have to get used to them."

"What if I make them up to you with Matt kisses?" he said with a wry grin.

She laid her hands on his shoulders and urged him close. "I think that's a deal I can live with."

"Glad to hear that," he said and sealed the deal with his kiss.

* * * * *

Look for more books in New York Times
bestselling author Caridad Piñeiro's
South Beach Security: K-9 Division series
when Escape the Everglades *goes on sale next month,*
only from Harlequin Intrigue!